Whi

- Rudyard Kipling's If.
ı greg Piano Concerto u
A minor

White Lies

J.C.Burke

Lothian
BOOKS

For my mother, Helen Burke, 1932–1985.
Death is just a physical absence, words live on.

Acknowledgments

For their encouragement, generosity, advice and input, the author would like to thank the following: Simone 'Reg' Begg; Chris Bender from Barrenjoey High School; Peter Brockhoff; David Burke; Margaret Burke; Gary Crew and the ASA mentorship program; Luke Cowan; Sam Egan Handshapes; Harry Girdler; Jai Israel; Peter Sheely Surfboards; Helen Chamberlin, publisher; Cathy Smith, editor; Susan Stitt; and last but certainly not least, the very patient Nicholas, Victoria and Michael Shehadie.

The poem on pp. 184–85 is *If* by Rudyard Kipling, 1865–1936.

Thomas C. Lothian Pty Ltd
132 Albert Road, South Melbourne, Victoria 3205
www.lothian.com.au

Copyright © J.C. Burke 2002
First published 2002

National Library of Australia
Cataloguing-in-Publication data:

Burke, J.C.
White lies.

For young adults.
ISBN 0 7344 0374 7.

1. Boys – Fiction. I. Title.
(Series: Lothian YA fiction).

A823.4

Cover design by Michelle Mackintosh
Cover photograph by Susan Stitt
Text design by John van Loon
Printed in Australia by Griffin Press

I am the master of my fate
I am the captain of my soul

– From *Invictus*
William Ernest Henley
1849–1903

chapter one

HE'D lift me onto the bonnet of the car and we'd watch the waves.

'You gotta study the swell, Mitch. You don't want to just go running in,' he'd say. 'You gotta learn to respect the sea. She can be your best mate or your worst nightmare.'

He'd light a rollie and we'd sit there staring.

'See that,' he'd say, his tanned arm out-stretched, his nuggetty fingers pointing. 'There's a rip, smooth water, no breaks. Dangerous for a swimmer, Mitch, but it can help you get out through the break.'

He'd watch some more, his blue eyes squinting to get a better view.

'You gotta remember, Mitch, if you get caught in a rip don't panic and don't swim against it, just go with the flow. Even the really bad rips come to an end. You understand?'

'Yes, Grandpa,' I'd reply.

∿∿∿

'Surf never sleeps,' sang Paul as he ripped the sheets off, revealing me in all my morning glory.

'Yeah, all right,' I said, pulling the sheet back. 'Give us a sec, will ya?'

'Bit tired, are you, mate?'

'Yeah, just a bit.'

'That'll teach you to hang out till all hours of the night.'

'Don't need the lecture, Paul,' I replied, trying to sound like my mother.

'Yeah, well your mother asked what time you got in and I said eleven o' clock, so no smart-arse talk to your ol' grandfather.'

'Wasn't much after that,' I mumbled, searching under my bed for a t-shirt. My best mate Harley had a party and it was a total chick fest. They were lucky I came home at all.

Paul chucked me the t-shirt I was looking for. 'It was two-thirty, Mitch,' he replied.

'What's an old bloke like you doing up then anyway?' I chuckled.

It was my new way of stirring Paul; since his fifty-sixth birthday he'd become all sensitive and had started saying, 'It's time to act my age' in this really serious voice. But he was perfect the way he was and I reckon deep down he knew that. I mean, what other grandfather'd drag you out of bed every morning at six a.m. to go surfing?

ʃ ʃ ʃ

'All right for some,' Mum said as she walked past with her mops and buckets.

'Need a hand, Liz?' Paul asked.

'Yeah, ta, Dad. Can you bring the vacuum cleaner out to the car?'

He went off to get it and I took the mops and buckets from her and followed outside.

'How come you're working on a Sunday?' I asked as I chucked them in the boot of her beat-up 1986 Mazda.

'The Richardsons had a wedding at their place last night. I said I'd come by this morning and clean up.'

'Sunday rates, I hope?' Paul said as he carried the vacuum to the car, the hose wound around his neck like some Indian snake charmer.

'Paul, don't start,' Mum said, slamming the boot. She always said his name in a firm way when she wanted to cut the conversation – a habit she'd acquired from him even though he seemed oblivious to it.

'I just don't like to think of that fancy family with all their money ripping you off.'

I saw Mum shoot him a hairy glare.

'OK,' Paul replied, shutting her door. 'Going to get you a new car one of these days.'

She leaned out and kissed him on the cheek. 'Yeah sure, Dad. Have a good surf, guys.'

They'd been a tight circle since my grandma died – Mum, her big sister Sue and Grandpa. Then there'd been the last sixteen years of just Mum, Grandpa and me. Even when they're silent I'm sure they're still communicating. I just don't know what about and come to think of it, maybe I don't want to know.

We zipped up each other's wetsuits and carried our boards to the beach.

～～～

The morning was fresh. We'd enjoyed a last burst of summer but the end of April had delivered the drop in temperature we'd all been dreading. At least the footpath had cooled down. Now we could cruise down the street instead of doing the Mexican hop.

'G'day,' we nodded to the early-bird surfers on their way home to bacon and eggs.

'Nice morning,' Paul muttered to the old girls out walking the dogs.

The hibiscuses were still out in their tropical blooms and the scent of frangipani lingered faintly in the air. It was a tease, enough to remind you of the summer just had, the parties, the waves, the chicks, the freedom, but faint enough to let you know that it was coming to an end and there were three long terms of school left.

We turned the corner into Surf Parade. The cliff

out the back. Paul had a big shed where he made all his surfboards, entertained his mates and used to sleep.

The shed always smelt of Paul's rollies mixed with the dust from the sanding machine. That room could be moved anywhere in the world, yet I swear if I was led in blindfolded I would still recognise it.

'Hey, Mitch,' Paul called. 'Come and meet Simon.'

'G'day, Mitch,' said Simon with a firm handshake.

He was shorter than he looked in photos and was pretty pumped. I should start doing some weights, I thought.

'Paul going to make you a board?' I asked.

'Yeah, a couple of small wave boards. The last one he made for me was magic.'

'Cheers, boys,' Paul said, raising his tinnie.

'Yeah, cheers,' we echoed.

'So you're off to Hawaii now?' Paul asked.

'Yeah, you ever surfed there?' Simon asked.

'About thirty-two years ago,' laughed Paul. 'Before you were even born, mate.'

Paul had never surfed overseas again. His wife got sick after he returned from that trip and died eighteen months later. She was only twenty-four. Paul was left to look after Mum and Aunty Sue, who were five and six years old. He still surfed, but only around home, where he was the local hero. It was around then that he got into making boards. I hate thinking about that time and how bad it must have been for him. Everyone says he was a world-class surfer and he still had all the newspaper clippings and photos to prove it. Sometimes when we talked about it he'd say, 'I just loved the waves, Mitch. I didn't care if I won a trophy or not, I just loved the waves.' And I knew that was true.

'You mix some air in your wave?' Paul asked.

'Try to,' Simon laughed.

'Seems to be the thing these days, doesn't it, Mitch?'

'Pretty awesome stuff,' was all I managed to say when what I really wanted to do was to grab him around the neck and yell, 'Show me how to do them, you sick maestro.'

He must have read my mind as he said, 'You got to have plenty of speed. That's the secret. You got to be going really fast.'

'I've been mucking around but haven't had much success,' I offered.

'Good mate, good.'

I found myself grinning and nodding in appreciation.

'Mitch's becoming a pretty good surfer,' Paul said. 'I reckon he'll be able to do that air stuff too if he keeps practising.'

'Dunno.' I could feel myself going red. God, I must have looked such a dickhead.

'Your grandad's right,' Simon said. 'Just keep

practising your moves and have a good time, that's what it's all about. I hear they're holding the junior titles at Kirra in March next year.'

'Yeah?' said Paul.

'How old are you, Mitch?' Simon asked.

'I'll be seventeen in September.'

'Do you compete much?'

'I try to.'

'Well, why don't you think about that? Paul'd know if you're good enough.'

I was taking in every single word. My ultimate dream was to be a pro surfer. Surfing was my life – I didn't know anything else, nor did I want to. I needed the water, needed to feel the strength of the waves as they carried me to another space. It's who I am. It's part of me.

two

H E'D lift me onto the bench in his workshed and show me the board he was working on.

'This is called a mal, or a longboard,' he'd say. 'In Hawaii in the old days they used to be made from huge pieces of wood.'

He'd rub the board with his tough freckled hands, his fingertips sparkling with particles of glass and sand.

'The shape and thickness are what's most important,' he'd say as he pinched the sides of the board and ran his palm along the outline. 'These are called the rails.'

'Do you like it, Mitchy?' he'd ask.

I'd nod my head in approval.

'Will I make you a board one day?'

'Yes please, Grandpa,' I'd reply.

~~~

'Mitchell, don't forget your lunch.' Mum chucked me a jumbo paper bag.

'Thanks.' Great catch.

'Are you working at the chemist this arvo?'

'Mum, you're getting that Alzheimer's thing,' I said. 'I already told you I'm not working Mondays any more.'

'Good,' she said with satisfaction. 'You can do some homework when you get home from school.'

'Depends.'

'On what?' she asked suspiciously.

'The waves,' I slipped in.

'*Mi-itch*,' I heard her call as I bolted out the front door.

I ran out the gate, shoved my lunch in my bag, swung it over my shoulder and jumped on my skateboard. No time to check out the surf – time for school, eighteen months to go and counting. I didn't really know what I wanted to do when I left, except surf, of course. A mate of Paul's had offered me an apprenticeship as a plumber but I reckon I'd rather hold a gun to my balls than go putting my arm down toilets all day. I mean, that is disgusting. Mum and Paul went on about what a great opportunity it is, blah, blah, blah, so to keep them off my case I agreed to think about it.

'Hey, Mitch, what've you got first?'

Harley was standing by the school gate in big goofy glasses.

'Dig your shades, mate,' I said.

He gave them a jiggle. He was definitely one of

the cool cats of the school. Some of the lefties called him a fashion victim, but they didn't know him. He was easy to knock because he stood out.

'I got maths,' I answered. 'How about you?'

'Geography, but I was thinking of giving it a miss.'

'Are you avoiding Angie?' I asked.

'She's hassling me all the time,' he whined. 'I mean, why can't some chicks accept that the end is the end?'

'Does she still want to get back together?'

'Yeah, but I keep telling her it's over and she just doesn't get it, man.'

'You're just too good,' I teased.

'It's not funny,' moaned Harley. 'It's starting to really give me the shits. I mean, when you broke up with that Vanessa chick she didn't keep hassling you.'

'That's 'cause she dumped *me*, dickhead!'

That was typical Harley being in his own Harley world, not even aware his best mate was the dumpee and not the dumper. Without sounding completely gay, Harley was good looking – he knew it and so did the girls. Angie had had the hots for him for ages before they finally got together and was devastated now they'd busted up after six months (a record for Harley). I knew all this because Angie and I were good mates and we talked a lot. I don't even think Harley knew that.

'Here she comes,' whispered Harley. 'I'm off.'

'Low,' I said under my breath. Exit Harley to my right, enter Angie to my left.

'G'day,' I said as brightly as I could manage.

'Hi, Mitch.' I watched her eyes follow Harley through the quadrangle. 'Look's like he's avoiding me again.'

I noticed her bottom lip quivering. Great, she's going to cry.

'He had to go up the shops,' I offered pathetically. Why was I making excuses for him? That was the one bad thing about Harley – he never did his own dirty work.

'Bastard,' whispered Angie and she burst into tears. 'I just don't know what happened. What did I do? I thought everything was going fine.'

I stood there feeling like a jerk. The tears were splashing onto Angie's cheeks, washing all the eye-liner off her eyes and onto her face. I tried not to look.

'Has he said anything to you, Mitch? You're his best friend.'

'Nah,' I lied. I wished she had a tissue so she could wipe all the black stuff off her face. Now her nose was running and she was doing these big gross snorts. The bell rang.

'Got to go,' I said.

'OK,' said Angie. She was looking tragic.

'Ange, you want to skip class and go down to the skate bowl?'

I seriously couldn't leave her like that.

'Yeah, Mitch. That'd be good.'

Angie and I walked down the bush track. You could either go left to the beach or right to the skate bowl. No matter what time or day it was, there were always kids hanging out there – avoiding school, parents, whatever they didn't want to face – but today we were the first there. We sat on the railing and Angie lit a smoke. She'd managed to clean up her face and pull herself together.

'So what did you do the rest of the weekend?' I asked.

'Babysat for the Richardsons. They had a big wedding at their house.'

'Yeah, I know. My mum told me.'

'God, have you been to their house?'

'Once, ages ago.'

'It's huge. It's like a hotel or something. The biggest decision of the night was which loo to use.'

'Yeah?'

'Diana was one of the bridesmaids. She looked amazing. I could not believe it.'

'Yeah, my mum said she looked all right.'

'All right! She looked beautiful – and I reckon she knew it. She actually managed to say hi, stuck-up cow. Why are some people like that?'

'Dunno,' I said. 'I s'pose they reckon they're better than us.'

'Yeah,' agreed Angie.

There was silence for a while and I noticed Angie getting restless.

'Mitch,' she began, 'is Harley seeing someone else?'

'Nah,' I said. 'I think his oldies are hassling him about the study.' Jesus, she'll never swallow that.

'Oh.'

Please, no more questions on that topic.

'Did he tell you that?'

'He mentioned it,' I mumbled. Harley's right. Chicks don't give up.

'Oh.'

I could hear the waves and could even taste a bit of salt. I noticed the wind had turned offshore from this morning. If the swell's anything like yesterday the surf should be pumping again by this arvo.

'Don't you reckon, Mitch?'

I'd gone to planet surf while Angie had still been raving on. 'Sorry?'

'That Harley's hard to talk to?' she repeated. 'I mean, he's in his own world.'

'Yeah, that's true.'

'It's different with you, Mitch. We've always been able to talk.'

I must have been truly entrenched in planet surf because it was only then that I realised Angie had moved up real close to me and was looking right at me – I mean, really looking at me.

'You like me, don't you, Mitch?'

Hang on! I didn't see this coming. I like Angie – she's a good mate – but she's always been Harley or some other bloke's girlfriend.

'I've always liked you, Mitch.'

She touched my face and kissed me softly on the lips, her mouth just open, her eyes just closed. As she pulled away she looked at me and smiled.

'That's the bell,' she whispered. 'We better go.'

Bell? What bell? I didn't hear the bell. We walked back to school in silence.

chapter three

HE'D hold the board counting one, two, three and push me onto a wave.

'Paddle! Paddle!' he'd call.

I'd pretend my arms were flippers and I'd move them as fast as I could make them go and up I'd stand, riding the white water, feeling like a super hero.

'Yahoo,' I'd hear him cry.

'Was I good, Grandpa?' I'd ask later as we hosed our boards down.

'You were the best,' he'd laugh and I'd want to get out there and try it all again.

∿∿∿

I didn't need to check out the surf on the way home. By the look of the guys heading towards the beach with their sticks I could tell it was on. The afternoon had not let me down. My day at school had been weird. Second period was physics and Mr Drummond sprung a test on us, sneaky bastard.

My head was still spinning after Angie's little surprise and I found it hard to concentrate. Was I feeling a bit horny or totally freaked out? Even lunch felt strange as I was having trouble looking Harley in the eye (not that it mattered with him in those shades). It was probably the only time I was glad to hear Tim crapping on. He saved me from having to open my mouth. Angie was nowhere to be seen. I figured if I stuck by Harley I'd be safe.

Mum was out the back with Paul when I got home. I snuck in, dumped my bag, grabbed my gear and bolted to the beach. There was a major wind-chill factor happening and I froze as I undressed, but I knew that bit of pain was going to be worth it. The sand almost felt like ice as I jumped up and down trying to warm up, but oh what beauty to my eyes – the surf was cranking and how!

The tide was low, the water a clear blue, the wind freezing but light and offshore. I watched a set of quality waves probably four foot cresting and breaking graciously, allowing the surfer an incredible pick of right and left handers. A few more sets like that and I'd be laughing. I jumped in and began paddling, nose-diving under the waves as I made my way out to the line-up. There were three others sitting on their boards waiting for the perfect wave, four specks in a vast ocean. I took slow deep breaths and enjoyed the moment as I waited my turn.

I ran all the way home and dived into the hottest shower. I stood there while the steam and heat defrosted my aching body. I bent over, feeling the water massage my back then flow off my shoulders. My mind drifted off to Angie, that look she gave me and the soft press of her lips against mine. My body obediently followed.

I'd never really thought about Angie in that way; other girls for sure, but never Angie. I felt drained yet contented. Great surf, good tug, a big feed and I'll be ready for bed.

The old girl stood at the door of my bedroom. I knew she was pissed off with me for disappearing.

'I'm not even going to ask where you've been.'

'Best waves for ages, Mum.'

'You said that yesterday, Mitch.'

'OK,' I relented. 'I'll do some work tonight.'

'Good, you can start now.'

She closed the door. I was going to do some work but a quick snooze was needed before I started. You know, recharge the batteries. But sometimes things don't work out like you plan.

The next couple of days I managed to get away with just the occasional hi and bye to Angie. She'd obviously stopped hassling Harley as he'd stopped whining about her. The swell had dropped – good for me as I had to work after school at the chemist and Mum was happy too as I'd caught up on my homework.

Working at the chemist was a complete bludge – all I had to do was ride around on my skateboard delivering the local prescriptions, and there were usually only three of them. I'd go and see Mrs Mayer, whose husband had one of those diseases where you can't breathe properly. I'd never actually seen him, but I could usually hear him coughing and hoiking in his room. Mrs Mayer always loaded me with chocky biscuits and occasionally got me to change a light globe.

The next delivery was bandages and dressing stuff for Mrs Papos. She had these dirty big ulcers on her legs which you could smell as soon as she opened the door. She always asked if I wanted to come in for some afternoon tea but I don't think my nasal passages could handle it.

Then there was Mr Howarth at the retirement village. He liked to talk about his 'dicky ticker', which cracked me up. When I'm finished I usually go and check out the waves or have a skate at the bowl and see a few mates then head back to the chemist for the last five minutes, but Mr Howarth was in hospital so I got back earlier than usual.

'Anything else you want me to do?' I asked Mrs Tran, the pharmacist.

'No, you can have an early mark, Mitch. Thanks for your help.'

'OK, see you tomorrow.'

'Oh, hang on, Mitch,' Mrs Tran called. Not so

speedy, I thought. 'I almost forgot. Your grandad wants these.'

She passed me a small package wrapped in white paper.

'What are they?' I said, trying to look through the paper.

'Pain killers,' Mrs Tran answered. 'He said his legs have been aching at night and I think he said his shoulder's sore too.'

'First I've heard,' I replied.

I took the box of tablets and set off home. That was the last I thought of it.

On the way I saw Angie and Jade. After school they worked at the local supermarket as check-out chicks. It used to be good for getting a discount on stuff but the manager started getting sus, which put an end to that.

'Hey, Mitch,' they waved.

I picked up my skateboard and crossed the road to meet them. I noticed Angie go red when I said hi.

'You going to Tim's on Saturday night?' Jade asked. Tim had the perfect parents – always away.

'Yeah, are you going?' I tried to make it sound like a general inquiry.

'For sure,' said Jade. 'What about you, Angie?'

As if Jade wouldn't know what Angie was doing every minute of the day. They were virtually joined. I stared at my trainers.

'I have to babysit.' Angie sounded disappointed and when I looked up she was looking at me all sad and droopy.

'Too bad,' I said, not really sure if I meant it or not.

'Are you babysitting your brothers or someone else?' asked Jade.

'My brothers.'

'Well, Tim's is only around the corner. Why can't you come after they've gone to sleep?'

'Jade!' Angie shrieked. 'Like imagine if Mum and Bill got home and I wasn't there? My life would be over – I mean totally over.'

'Just a suggestion,' Jade said. 'Like don't bite my head off.'

We reached Jade's street, now it was the two of us. We walked amongst an awkward silence. Why is it like that? You're good mates with a chick, then something happens and all of a sudden you got nothing to talk about. We reached my place.

'See ya,' I said.

Angie hesitated. I could tell she was hanging to say something or hoped that I would. I just wanted to get inside.

'Mitch?' She was twisting her brown curls around one of her fingers. 'On Saturday night maybe, that's if you want to – um – maybe you could come and visit me for a while.'

'Um, yeah maybe,' I replied.

'OK,' she smiled. 'See you tomorrow.'

'Yep.'

That was the best I could do.

chapter *four*

HE brought out his 'magic mal' from the old days and put it on the grass next to the frangipani tree. I giggled as I watched him pretend to surf. He stepped forwards and backwards, walking his plank with the ease and grace of a dancer.

He crouched down, pretending to dip his head into the water and as he stood up shook his hair and wiped his nose, his expression always focused as if he was doing the real thing.

I'd clap and shout, 'Do it again, Grandpa. Toes on the nose, toes on the nose.'

And he would go faster this time, his feet running up and down the length of the board as if it were on fire, but all the time displaying that perfect balance and control he had mastered.

'It's all about balance, Mitch. Balance is everything,' he'd say, his arms stretched in front of him. 'Not only in surfing, in life too.'

I'd nod. Just knowing him made me understand.

I reckon living close to the sea you develop an instinct as to what the conditions are like out there. We don't have an ocean view so I rely on my other senses. The direction of the wind as well as its strength and smell, the sound of the waves hitting the shore, the shape of the clouds and the colour of the sky. As winter approaches, the clues change again, but you still get a hunch. At least I do.

Saturday morning I had one of those hunches, the swell had died earlier in the week but it felt like it was back. I shuffled down to the back of the house where Paul and I had our favourite morning toilet. Mum referred to it as the room for 'men's business'. I sat on the loo and flicked through my latest surf mag. There was a big article on Simon Dobson. They were calling him the 'Messiah of the waves' – now that's a title I could live with.

'Hey, Paul,' I shouted from the loo. 'Have you seen this article on Dobbo?'

'Paul?'

God, I hope he hasn't gone down without me. He prides himself on being one of those real early birds. You know 'early to bed, early to rise', all that crap.

'Hey, Paul?' I called again.

His bedroom door was closed.

'Paul?' I knocked gently on the door. 'You awake, mate?'

He was lying on his back, an arm and a leg hanging off the bed, his mouth wide open. For some reason it unsettled me seeing him like this. I sat on the end of the bed and gave his leg a shove. I noticed a clump of tiny grey bruises on his lower leg. The box of pain killers I'd brought home a few days before had been ripped open and little pieces of foil littered his bedside table.

'Paul?' I gave his leg another shove, not so rough this time.

The frangipani tree outside his bedroom window had just a few flowers left; smooth white curled petals splashed with yellows and oranges. It had always been Paul's favourite tree and when Aunty Sue left home he moved out of his workshed and into her room.

'I love this tree,' he'd say. 'Its perfume works like a sleeping potion.'

One, two, three – only four flowers left.

'Are you waiting for your morning bottle?'

Paul was awake, I heard myself sigh with relief.

'My what?' I said.

'Your morning bottle. Every morning till you were nearly four you'd sit on the end of your bed holding out your bottle and demanding a refill.'

'Did I have a bottle till I was four?'

'Yep,' Paul laughed. 'Just another little fact your mother and I decided to keep from you. All for your psychological well-being of course.'

'You were dead to the world.'

'I took a few tablets about five a.m. They must have knocked me out.'

'Mrs Tran told me your legs were keeping you awake.'

Paul sprang out of bed, almost knocking me to the floor.

'Nothing wrong with my legs.'

'You want to check out the surf?' I asked.

'Let's go, buddy boy.'

We were in luck. The Easter swell had returned in May! Our beach had one of the most consistent breaks in New South Wales or maybe even Australia or maybe the universe. The map refers to it as 'Kollendina Beach' but us locals just say 'Kollie'. They reckon it means curling water. The sea spray leapt up in excitement as we turned the corner into Surf Parade. Sometimes I feel like it's saying, 'Hurry up, get in and join the party.' At times its impatience mirrors mine.

'It's an absolute gala, fellas,' said Rod Thornton, a big cheesy grin plastered on his face, his fat gut bulging out of his wet suit.

'I was wondering where you were, Paul.'

'Slept in,' answered Paul. 'You going to the club tonight?'

'I'm taking my new bird,' Rod said, his grin expanding past his ears.

'Way to go, mate,' I laughed.

'Mitchell, the day I can't get to the club and have a good sniff around is the day the good Lord can take me,' Rod declared. 'Ain't that right, Paul?'

'Too right, mate, too right,' Paul agreed. 'See you tonight.'

'Rod's always got a new chick,' I said.

'As long as I've known Rod it's always been surfing and sheilas; two wives, six kids and eight grandchildren later it hasn't changed,' said Paul, taking the rollie from behind his ear. 'Yep, Rod and the tide – two things I can always be sure of.'

Paul took a deep drag then blew the smoke out in one steady breath.

'It's a funny thing,' he muttered.

'What is?' I said.

'Getting old,' he answered softly.

'Like how do you mean?' I said.

'How long can I keep doing this?' he said, pointing to the sea. 'I mean, it'll all come to an end one day.'

'You're being morbid,' I said.

'Try realistic,' Paul answered. He stood up, picked up his board and walked to the edge of the surf. 'You coming?' he called.

I watched as Paul eased himself onto his board and paddled out. I don't purposely sit there and watch him – half the time I don't even realise I am. But the grace and power he cuts in his big turns on a longboard are as awesome as watching a young gun cut fast snappy turns. His gift was a sense of the wave and its rhythm, granting him a style that was famous for its elegance and fluidity. He was a natural sportsman and that was why myself and others were often drawn to this sight.

My grandfather in his humility would say, 'Any person of any age can ride a longboard.'

I spotted one of the locals, Jed Travis, a powerful and aggressive surfer who dropped in on anyone and any wave just for the heck of it. He was repeating Year 11 and he wasn't happy about it. He already had a reputation as being as big a dickhead in the water as out. He stopped when he saw me.

'You gonna sit there and watch your old grandaddy all day?' he said with a smart-arse look on his ugly dial. He couldn't help himself. His mission in life was to cause aggravation. I ignored him – anyone with half a brain ignored him. He said it again, so I stood up (lucky I was much taller than him), got my board and walked off into the ocean.

'You tosser,' I heard him say.

I paddled out to where Paul was.

'He's a loser, that Jed Travis,' I said.

'Yeah,' Paul agreed.

'Yeah,' I said.

'Shame,' added Paul. 'He's becoming a good surfer.'

But the conversation was stopped by a beautiful wave that came through the break, sledging over to a three-foot spitting barrel that I pulled into.

I sat on the front steps and waited for Harley. He was typically late. 'Harley time,' I called it. I hadn't decided whether I was going to visit Angie tonight; in fact, I hadn't really given it much thought at all except I did shave a bit of gristle off my chin.

I knew I kind of wanted to see her but at the same time I wasn't really that bothered and I definitely didn't want any hassles with Harley. He's my best mate. Sometimes blokes can be funny. They decide they don't want a particular chick but as soon as someone else gets off with her they decide they want her back. I was still having a bit of trouble thinking of Angie in that way. I mean, she was pretty enough and had nice big tits I wouldn't mind getting my hands on. To be honest I've probably given that the most thought. I'll see what Tim's party's like, make up my mind then. Harley came strolling down the street at a leisurely pace.

'Hey,' he said.

'G'day,' I said. 'Like your blue hair.'

'Want some?' Harley pulled a spray can out of his jacket pocket.

'Nah,' I laughed. 'I think I'll go au naturale.'

'Tim and Reece are spraying their hair fluoro pink.'

'The tossers,' I said.

'Hope Angie hates my blue hair,' Harley said, running his hands through it.

'She's not going to be there,' I replied.

'She's not?' Harley sounded surprised. I decided not to say anything else.

'You want to go to the bottlo?'

'You got any ID?' I asked.

'Nah,' answered Harley. 'I'll be right.' Harley could easily pass for eighteen, but sometimes there was some straight dickhead at the counter who insisted on checking everyone's ID.

'I'm going to get a burger,' I said. 'You want one?'

'Yeah, but no onions,' winked Harley. Dirty bugger, his mind's always in his daks.

Harley went off to try his luck at the bottle shop and I went to the milkbar.

Trev the milkbar owner knew everyone; he'd had the shop for fourteen years. He'd seen the changes and witnessed people come and go. If there was anything you wanted to know, Trev was your man.

'What can I do for you, Mitch?'

'Two works burgers,' I said. 'One without onion.'

'That's for young Harley, eh?' laughed Trev.

I sat on the bench outside and waited. I zipped up my jacket. The evenings were starting to get cold much earlier. A navy-blue four-wheel drive with P plates pulled up, a woman with big dark glasses slumped in the passenger's seat. I saw the back of a girl with straight blonde hair nearly to her waist slam the driver's door and run into the chemist across the road.

The woman in the passenger's seat was now

leaning forward. I noticed her back and head convulsing like she was spewing – unless you can have a fit
sitting up. I was wondering if I should go and see if
the lady was OK when I saw the girl come out of the
chemist. God, it was Diana Richardson. She gave me
a look that assured me she didn't want my company,
got back in the car and drove off with the woman in
the front still convulsing. I turned around and saw
Trev standing by the door of his milkbar, our burgers
in his hand.

'Tragic,' he muttered.

I handed him the money, took our burgers and
went to see if Harley had done well.

～～～

We walked into the usual scene at Tim's. Loud music,
a couple of empty pizza boxes on the table, a group of
Year 10 girls sitting together, Reece and some chick
pashing on the couch, Tim running around already
pissed with his fluoro-pink hair and red face and a
group on the verandah sitting around a bong. Harley
gave me the beer and went out to pull a cone. I wandered into the kitchen where Jade, her sister Sophie
and Toby were sitting around the table. I sat down
and opened my twist-top. The first few sips of cold
lager are always the best. Toby and I swapped tales on
the day's surfing while Jade and Sophie sat there and
chain-smoked. Later Jade cornered me in the hallway.

I knew what it was going to be about.

'Are you going to visit Angie?' she asked, her blue nails tapping on the wall.

'Dunno. Maybe,' I said.

'You know she really likes you.'

'Yeah?' I wish I knew how that was meant to make me feel.

Harley appeared. He grabbed Jade from behind and she squealed.

'Got any matches, gorgeous?' he asked.

'Yeah, your face with my bum,' she laughed.

I left them wrestling in the hallway and wandered out the door and before I'd really thought about it I had turned the corner into Angie's driveway.

chapter *five*

HE'D take me to the surf club every Saturday afternoon.

We'd sit by the window away from a large black-and-white photo of him that hung on the wall.

Alice the waitress would bring over a beer for Paul and a lemonade with a scoop of vanilla ice-cream for me.

Everyone would stop and say hi and sometimes I'd hear people whisper, 'Isn't that Paul Davies?'

Once when I was on my way back from the toilet I heard a man say to his son, 'See that man sitting there by the window? He'll be remembered as one of the greatest surfers of his time.'

When I repeated this to my grandfather, he smiled through his clear blue eyes and said, 'I'd just like to be remembered as a good man.'

ᔕᔕᔕ

I was aware of my heart pounding as I rang the doorbell of Angie's house – it felt like you could actually see it through my jacket. Maybe this was the beginning of a heart attack. I thought about doing the bolt, but before I could psych my legs into action Angie was standing at the door.

'Hi,' she said, leaning against the doorway, a big smile on her face.

'G'day,' I croaked.

She was wearing a pair of faded blue jeans that barely sat on her hips and a tight black jumper that was cut off just above her belly button. She looked a lot hotter than I'd expected and it kind of caught me off guard. I followed her inside.

'Do you want a drink?'

'No, thanks.' The couple of beers I had at the party were starting to brew a warm fuzz in my head.

'Do you want something to eat?'

'I'm right, thanks.' I had stood in this kitchen a thousand times with Angie and sometimes with Jade and Harley laughing, having food fights, mixing drinks and mucking around, but never like this. It felt weird. I followed her into the living room. She turned off the TV and flopped onto the couch. I stood next to the TV flicking through the guide, trying to make out like I was interested in what was on the box.

'What's happening at Tim's?' she asked.

'Usual scene, not much,' I replied, still with my head in the guide.

'You want to watch something?' she said.

'Yeah OK.' I turned the TV back on. I badly needed some background noise. I sat down on the couch next to her.

'Was Harley there?'

'Yeah,' I said. 'He sprayed his hair blue.'

'What a wanker,' she said. 'You know, Mitch, I'm so over him.'

What was I meant to say to that? I settled with nothing.

'Have you started your English essay?' she asked.

'Not yet,' I replied.

'Me neither,' she sighed. 'Did you go for a surf today?'

'Yep,' I nodded. Angie was a chronic nail biter and I noticed she was virtually eating her fingers.

'Is something wrong, Mitch?' I could feel her desperately trying to make eye contact.

'Is it Harley? Are you feeling funny about, you know, you and me and him and stuff? Because like I said before I'm totally, I mean totally over him.' She sounded convincing.

'Yeah?' I could hear my foot tapping on the leg of the coffee table. 'I guess I feel a bit funny about it, you being Harley's ex and everything and you know we've always been mates.'

'Do you like me?' She had finally won eye contact and I had a hunch she wasn't going to let it go.

'Yeah,' I replied. 'Of course I like you.'

'Then what's the problem?' she laughed.

She had little brown freckles on her nose and her teeth were white and straight. I leant over and kissed her. She put one hand firmly around my neck and pulled me closer. I opened my mouth and felt the warmth of her tongue circling mine.

She slid down the couch and pulled me on top of her. My legs hung off the end of the armrest. I put one foot on the floor to steady myself. It wasn't very comfortable but I couldn't have cared less. I ran my hands over her jumper and shuddered as I felt her tits for the first time, their roundness moulding into my palms. She lifted her head and I cradled her neck with one hand; she was kissing me deeply and running her hand along my leg.

'You're so lovely and tall,' she whispered.

∿∿∿

I didn't feel like going back to the party so I walked home. It was nearly eleven o'clock and Trev's was still open so I went in and bought some chips and a coke.

'Good party?' he asked.

'Yeah, it was OK.' That man had to know everything.

I walked through the skate bowl and sat on the railing eating my chips. It felt good being alone out here. God, Angie's had gone better than I thought it would. I felt pretty turned on with her but managed an escape before things got too complicated. I didn't want to give her the wrong idea. She was heavily into relationships and let's just say I wasn't. I didn't know whether to say anything to Harley. I felt like I didn't really have to as Angie didn't heavy me about what 'the situation' was between us even though she seemed pretty keen. Don't make something out of nothing, Paul always says and besides, things usually work out for themselves.

I got up, chucked my can at the bin and missed. I walked over to pick it up and as I bent down I distinctly heard a rustling sound coming from the bushes. As I looked around, I got the feeling that someone or something was watching me. If I stood still I noticed there was silence, but as soon as I started to move I heard the same noise.

I tried it again. I walked a few steps, heard it, stopped and then there was nothing. I wasn't scared, I was curious. So again I walked a couple of steps, faked like I was going to stop, then bolted up to the bushes. The sound of twigs and leaves crunching under someone's foot was now very clear and I reached the bush just in time to see a figure flash by. I could've sworn it was a girl.

∫∫∫

The first Sunday of every month our surf club had a grommet comp. Paul and his mate Rod Thornton started the club about fifteen years ago. Surfing got a bit of a reputation as being an individual sport where you surf and compete for yourself only. Some of the oldies thought this was a pretty unhealthy attitude so they started the club and comps for young surfers like myself. Paul reckons kids need a sense of belonging and 'there's nothing wrong with a bit of tradition', he'd say.

The scene was pretty relaxed and gave us an opportunity to improve on our techniques and get some advice as well as check out the other competitors who were usually our mates, with the exception of Jed 'Dickhead' Travis and a few others. It was an early start – six-thirty a.m. – and after those few beers at Tim's and a restless sleep I felt pretty groggy.

It was chilly at that time of the morning and getting into my wetsuit reminded me of the old saying 'freeze the balls off a brass monkey' because that's what was happening to me. Each heat was twenty minutes and we had to wear coloured vests over our wetsuits to identify ourselves in the water. A few oldies judged, but mostly it was us scoring each other. Apparently they call that healthy competition.

Toby, Reece, a girl called Melissa and Jed were out first. The idea was to catch at least five good waves in the twenty-minute period. The more turns you made, the more points you got.

Paul passed me a clipboard and pen. 'You score this round for me, Mitch.'

'Why, what are you doing?'

'I told Jed I'd video him,' he said.

'That dickhead,' I said under my breath.

'Mitch,' Paul shot me a look. 'This is sport, mate, none of that thanks, at least not in our club.'

Paul was always fair and I admired him for it, but Jed Travis – give us a break. Unfortunately it was Jed and me who were picked as the seniors to surf in the high school comp. I say unfortunately because spending any time with him was just that.

I'd always hoped it would be me and Toby, but now Jed was repeating Year 11 it looked like I'd be stuck with him for another year.

It was choppy and the wind was onshore, blowing up the white water, but they – whoever *they* are – say it's good practice to try out your moves in junk surf.

Jed was the first to get on a wave and although it looked pretty bumpy out there he handled the waves well using lots of rail, gouging the face of the wave.

'Way to go,' I heard Paul shout.

The other guys and me looked at each other. It was a shame we had to score him on his surfing instead of his dickhead ability. That was the thing about Jed, his aggro personality also came out in the water. He attacked the wave like he owned it, making sure it never got the better of him. For that second I contemplated becoming an aggro bastard myself, but somehow I didn't think I could pull it off quite as well.

'You're in next, Mitch,' Rod said, chucking me a vest.

Paul was standing at the shore fiddling with the video camera. As I passed him he said quietly, 'You can do it as well as him, Mitch. Just remember: don't be intimidated.'

It was only Paul who knew that secret of mine.

I paddled out. 'He's right,' I said to myself. 'Don't be intimidated.'

I focused on the grey horizon ahead and repeated those three words over and over again. As I sat on my board waiting, I could see Paul still standing there by the shore, the video camera in position. A set came rolling in. The wind had turned slightly and in response the quality of the wave had improved. I knew I was in the best position to catch this one. I started to paddle, the strength in my arms giving me the speed I needed to stay in front of the break. I knew it was a heavier and faster wave than Jed had ridden and I wanted it. I drove the board hard, picking up speed. I cut a left-hand turn that was as fluid as it was fast. I could hear the gush of water rushing past me then spraying up before me in its defiance of gravity.

This was my power.

As I walked back up the sand I saw a smile resting gently on Paul's face and I knew I'd done OK. Mum had arrived and was busy barbecuing the snags and eggs – it was a way to make a bit of cash for the club.

'You want a sambo, Mitch?'

'Yeah, ta Mum,' I said, jumping up and down.

'Don't shake your mop all over me, I've had a wash today, thanks.'

'Sorry, ma.' It was a bad habit of mine.

'Come here and give me a kiss.'

I put my arms around her skinny frame. She was much younger than the other mothers. She was only seventeen when she'd had me. I bent down to kiss her and she tried to smooth down my hair like I was still a little boy.

'How did I get such a tall son with so much blond hair? You must be a throwback to the Vikings.'

'You forgot to mention good looking too,' I said.

'No, I didn't. Here,' she passed me my sandwich. 'Two dollars, please.'

'What!'

'Everyone has to pay.'

'OK, put it on my bill,' I mumbled, searching through the esky.

'The sauce is on the table, love.'

How is it that mothers know everything?

The wind had picked up and changed direction again, so by the time the third heat was due to start the surf was completely blown out.

'I think we'll call it a day,' announced Paul. 'Well done, everyone.'

I helped pack up and stuffed the leftover sausages down my throat while Mum and Paul chatted by the barbie.

'You guys crippled?' I said.

They looked up at me in horror as if they'd forgotten I was there.

'I said, are you guys crippled or something?'

Mum nodded her head and walked away. She looked upset.

'What?' I said. Had I put my foot in it?

'Don't worry,' Paul answered, putting his arms around my shoulders and giving me a squeeze.

'You're making me paranoid,' I said.

'You know, Mitch, I think it's time I made you a board. Custom made just for you, buddy. We'll design it together.'

'Really?' I said. 'That'd be cool.'

'How long till your seventeenth birthday?'

I counted on my fingers. 'About ten weeks.'

'Good. That'll give me time,' he replied. 'You're surfing well, Mitch, really well.'

chapter Six

H E looked at me with my black eye and bleeding nose. 'I hope the other boy looks worse,' he laughed.

I burst into tears and he wrapped his strong arms around me. It felt like this cocoon would keep the bad things out.

'Shhh,' he comforted, his voice soothing away my shame.

'He kept calling me a bastard,' I cried. 'He said his parents said I was.'

'A bastard just means someone whose mum and dad aren't married, it's a stupid word,' he said, gently dabbing the blood from my nose.

'But I don't have a dad.'

'I know, Mitch.'

'I've got you,' I said defiantly.

'Too right you do,' he said, a soft smile unfolding the creases in his face. 'You've got me forever.'

~~~

What's the big deal about Mondays? Everyone's meant to hate Mondays and yet in a psycho sort of way I love them. It's the beginning of a new week and anything could happen. Maybe the most awesome of all swells could hit Kollie, making it the week I catch that perfect wave. Who knows, the school could spontaneously combust, Simon Dobson may announce to the world he's my long lost big brother and just to top it off Mum could win Lotto. Optimism – it's my strength and it's bound to be my downfall.

Harley, Tim and Reece were hanging out by the lockers. I could hear Reece's account of a cuttie he executed on the weekend and could hear the others echoing, 'Sick. Awesome.' Reece was notorious for blowing things out of all proportion, but he could tell a great yarn.

'G'day, Mitch,' they mumbled in unison.

'Hey, what happened to you on Saturday night?' asked Tim, a bit too eagerly, I thought.

'Surprised you remember anything,' interrupted Reece. 'You were off your face, man.'

'I was not.'

'You're hopeless with your piss,' said Harley.

'And other things,' added Reece. Harley and him burst out laughing.

'Shut up,' said Tim, having a fair idea what they were on about.

While they crapped on I buried my head in my

locker, hoping they wouldn't come back to the original question. I'm pretty sure no one saw me slip out (except Jade, but she would've been on the lookout), but maybe my mistake had been not coming back to the party. Idiot. The bell rang signalling Monday morning assembly. I waited for them to wander off while I continued to shuffle around in my locker trying to look busy. I peered through the crack of the door to check that the coast was clear and spied Angie standing there.

'Hi,' she said.

'Yeah, g'day,' I answered.

'You going to assembly?'

'Yep,' I said trying to sound casual. 'I just gotta get this stuff sorted out in my locker.'

'It's OK,' she said, leaning into the locker. 'I can wait.'

I couldn't exactly say to her, 'No don't, 'cause I don't want my mates to see me with you,' so I shuffled my papers a bit more then said, 'OK, I'm ready.'

It was my guilt that was making me feel so paranoid. Ordinarily I wouldn't think anything of walking through the playground with Angie. Just be cool, I said to myself, even though I felt like I was walking out to a firing squad. The headmaster was up there talking about the 'blue awards' that are given out towards the end of the year. I got a sports one for surfing last year but I reckon Jed was tipped to get it this year. When he mentioned the surfing award, Angie squeezed my elbow. God, I wish she hadn't done that. The headmaster announced they were introducing a new award for dancing. There were a few sniggers in the crowd and I heard Jade say, 'I wonder who that will be? *Derrr.*'

'She got her driver's licence,' Angie whispered, knowing who Jade was referring to. 'She's driving around in some big flash four-wheel drive thinking like she's shit hot.'

'Yeah,' said Jade. 'I can just imagine.'

I didn't say anything about what I saw on Saturday night. Angie whispered something to Jade and they burst out laughing.

'Like somehow I don't think Diana's that sort of chick,' said Jade. 'Shame to waste the black leather seats though.'

Angie and Jade gave each other one of those all-knowing girl looks that I can never work out.

'What?' I said.

'Don't worry, Mitch,' Jade said, patting my arm. 'You're too nice a boy to know what we're saying.' And they burst out laughing again.

'Yeah, see ya,' I said.

I wandered back to class on my own feeling confused about the secret language of chicks.

'Mitch?' someone called.

I turned around and saw Tim. He was a big guy,

not so much fat as solid and being a ginger head couldn't handle too much of the sun.

'Wait up,' he panted. He'd been an asthmatic all his life and after a weekend of booze and fags he was wheezing. Tim didn't surf, he partied, and klepto-mania was his other hobby.

'You getting into Angie's daks?' he said, still a little breathless.

'Huh?' I said. He was a definite desperate.

'You and Angie, that's what I've heard.'

'You are a desperate,' I said to his face.

'Come on,' Tim urged. 'That's where you went the other night, wasn't it, you sly dog?'

'Piss off, you sicko,' I said, turning into my class-room.

I was late for class so I snuck in and took the closest seat at the back of the classroom. Bloody Tim and his big mouth, that's all I need. Everyone had *Othello* open. I leant across and whispered, 'What page number?'

'Nineteen,' she answered bluntly.

When I looked up to see who owned the unfriendly voice I saw Diana Richardson giving me that same cold look. There was something about her eyes – they were grey and blank like they didn't actu-ally belong to anyone. That's the only way I can describe it.

'Thanks,' I muttered, fumbling through my book.

⟋⟋⟋

Tim hassled me a few more times during the week and one of those times was in front of Harley. As always Harley seemed to be in his own head space, not really listening to what was going on, but as we walked home from school that arvo he caught me completely off guard. We were having our usual rugby league convo – Harley going on and on about all the great players Canberra had bought and me slagging them off. The fact that Harley's team was from another state disgusted me, but no matter how hard I tried to convert him I couldn't make him see the light.

'I love the Raiders, they're a class act.'

'Yeah, B class,' I stirred.

'So you're seeing Angie?' He said it like that.

'It's nothing really,' I replied.

'Jade reckons she really likes you.'

'I wouldn't know.'

'Mitch, I couldn't care less,' Harley said. 'I mean, I may have to smash up your face a little in public and all but between you and me I don't care, honest.'

'Well, you know if you did,' I started, 'I'd stop seeing her. I don't think it'd worry me.'

'Look, Angie's a good chick, Mitch, but you know what I reckon?'

'I got a feeling you're going to tell me.'

'I don't think she's your type, as a girlfriend that is.'

'Yeah well, what is my type, Dr Love?'

'You've got to find a girlfriend that shares your obsession with surfing or at least doesn't get the shits with it. You know how demanding chicks can be if you don't spend every second with them.'

'I don't know,' I said, thinking about the other thing he said. 'Do you really think I'm obsessed?'

'Look, some kids are christened Church of England, some are Buddhists, Jewish, Moslem whatever, but you, mate, you worship the God of Surf.'

I tried to imagine what the Surf God looked like. He'd be pretty laid back, that's for sure and I'm sure he'd be a bloke.

'I mean, look at Paul.' Harley was on a roll. 'His religion is surfing and the only thing you've ever said about your old man was that he was a surfer, so there you go.'

My 'old man' – I found it hard to wrap my mind around that one.

'You know that's all I really do know about him,' I said, almost to myself I think. 'And he's American.'

'God, I'd want to know everything about him,' Harley said.

'I really don't give him any thought,' I said. 'I guess I just don't feel the need.'

'Yeah, well you're lucky,' Harley said. 'See you tomorrow.'

I went inside feeling like I must have been a bit

weird, but that was the truth. I hardly ever thought about who my dad was or where he was. It was as simple as that.

I threw my bag in my room and went and raided the fridge. Mum was on the phone to Aunty Sue – I knew that 'cause all she was saying was, 'Yes, yes.' It was hard – verging on a physical impossibility – to get a word in with Sue. She lives in the country and works as one of those community nurses. I have my suspicions she's a dyke but Mum swears she's not.

'OK, I'll be there with Dad at three o'clock.' My god, she actually got eight words in. 'Yes, I'll tell him … Yes … Yes … OK … Yes … See you tomorrow.'

I stood there shoving a bread roll in my mouth.

'Is Sue coming down?' I mumbled.

'Don't eat with your mouth full,' Mum snapped.

'Sorry.' I swallowed the bread. 'Is Sue coming to stay?'

'Yes,' Mum answered. 'She's coming tomorrow.'

'Tomorrow? How come?'

'What do you mean how come? She wants to see her family, is that all right?' she snapped again.

'OK,' I said. 'Don't bite my head off.'

'Are you off to work?' she asked.

'Yeah,' I said.

'You want a lift? I have to pick Paul up in town.' She was sounding stressed.

'Nah, I'll walk.'

'OK.' She got her bag and left. God, she was in a weird mood, probably that time of the month. She gets a bit cranky then and I steer clear.

I got my skateboard and set off for the chemist run. Mrs Tran was busy filling the delivery bag with bottles of pills and bandages – it amazed me how her tiny hands worked so quickly.

'Hello, Mitch, how are you today?' she asked.

'Good, thanks,' I replied.

'Mr Howarth's back from hospital, his new script's in here,' she said, holding up the bag. 'Mrs Mayer's asked for some extra oxygen tubing too.'

I nodded my head.

'She's in a tizz about connecting it but I said I'm sure you'd help her.'

'Yep,' I nodded, wondering what chocky biscuits she'd bought this week.

'Oh, and don't leave without taking this home.' She held up another one of those packages wrapped in white paper, more pills for Paul.

The Mayers lived in a blue weatherboard cottage in the old part of Kollie.

The first time I went there I couldn't find the front door through the jungle. I needed a machete to hack my way through. I never leave their place on my own – there's always a couple of ticks on me or a leech and if the old dear raves on at the front door I get eaten alive by mozzies.

'Hello, Mitchell,' said Mrs Mayer, squelching around the house in gum boots. 'Did you bring the oxygen tubing?'

I took out the packet of thin green tubing from the bag. She trudged down the hallway.

'You're a wonderful boy,' she said, her voice trailing off. 'Come with me.'

'Where are you?' she called from her bedroom.

I stood at the doorway. I had never seen Mr Mayer, had never put a face to the horrible sounds of a man who couldn't breathe, and I wasn't sure I wanted to.

'Don't be shy,' Mrs Mayer called. 'He's in the shower.'

I felt ashamed of my fear and revulsion. The door to their tiny ensuite was half open and through the steam I could see a man, a frail man hunched over on a chair, his shoulders rising and falling with the effort of staying alive. I turned around to see Mrs Mayer wheeling an enormous cylinder towards me.

'Now the tubing needs to be connected here.' She pointed to a tiny valve.

As I connected it she chatted on, making me wonder if she'd forgotten her husband in the shower.

'I get pins and needles in my fingertips, which makes me so clumsy. See what happens when there isn't a man around the house? Everything goes to rack and ruin,' she sighed. 'Sickness and old age, it's a terrible curse, Mitch.'

I nodded, wondering what to say.

'Mr Mayer turned sixty last month,' she whispered. 'I don't think he'll see sixty-one.'

I couldn't wait to get out of there. I didn't even hang around for the chocky biscuits.

I delivered the rest of the stuff quickly. I'd seen enough old and sick people to last me the rest of the year. I hung out at the skate bowl, riding up and down, the noise of the wheels on the concrete numbing my brain. There was one thought I couldn't get rid of – Mr Mayer was only a few years older than Paul. I tried to imagine Paul like that and it made me feel horrible. I sat on the railing while the last of the afternoon light faded into a chilly dusk. I noticed a new bit of concrete had been poured to reinforce one of the loose railings. Someone had already inscribed their initials. I traced my finger around the letters D.R. that were set in this spot forever.

seven

H E took hold of my shoulders and steered me through the crowd. I knew he didn't want me to see the two men fighting but I could still hear them yelling and swearing.

'They got nothing better to do,' he said under his breath.

'What do you mean?' I asked.

He didn't answer but later on the way home he said, 'Mitch, it's so important to have something in your life that you love. Have a passion, something that you can really immerse yourself in, especially when times are tough. Something that feeds your soul and brings you peace within yourself. Without this you're like an aimless man trying to find what he hasn't lost.'

I knew then he'd answered my question.

～～～

Aunty Sue arrived and the ear bashing began. She got

home in the evening with the others and her chatter was as irritating as Mum and Paul's silence. I'd be kind if I said she'd put on a bit of weight – man, she'd stacked it on. It gave me a shock when she walked in and I quickly turned my head to hide the fact that my eyes had just popped out of their sockets.

'Hi, Mitch,' she said, giving me a peck on the cheek. 'How's it going?'

'Good,' I said, and backed away from her foul breath. What had she eaten for lunch?

'I hear you're doing lots of surfing,' she said, and helped herself to a beer.

'Yeah, just the usual,' I replied, knowing she wasn't really listening.

'You want a beer, Dad?' she called.

'Better not,' Paul said.

'It won't interfere with tomorrow,' Sue replied.

'Nah, better not,' he said.

'OK.' Sue slammed the fridge door and dumped herself on the couch, nearly sending the others catapulting off the other end.

'What's happening tomorrow?' I said.

I saw Paul, Mum and Sue exchange a look. One of those 'we know but we don't know if we should tell you' kind of looks. I waited to see if I would be let into their secretive adult world.

'Come on, I'll be seventeen soon,' I said, not meaning to reveal my thoughts out loud.

Sue looked at Paul and just as she was opening her mouth he put up his hand as if to stop her.

'I have to go for some tests tomorrow at RPA,' said Paul.

Royal Prince Alfred was the big hospital in the city. I knew that 'cause Mum watched some TV show about it every week and always ended up crying.

'What for?' I said.

'They're just checking me out to see why I'm off my tucker and my shoulder and legs are hurting, that's all.'

He lifted his legs in front of him. They were tanned and muscular, the legs of a fit man, a healthy man.

'Oh no,' I sighed.

'It'll be nothing,' Paul reassured.

'No, not that,' I said. 'I forgot to bring home those pills yesterday.'

'Mitch!' Mum snapped. 'Can't you think of someone else for once.'

'I forgot. All right, I'm sorry.'

'Yeah, yeah, you're always sorry,' Mum said sarcastically.

'Come on, Lizzy,' Paul said, putting his arm around his youngest daughter. She put her head on his shoulder and started to cry. Now I felt really bad.

'Sorry, Mum,' I said.

'No, I'm sorry, Mitch.' She got up off the couch and walked over to me. 'Give us a hug.'

I put my arms around her and again she cried. Somewhere down in my guts I knew she needed me like the way she sometimes needed Paul. I think it scared me because I didn't know if I could be as good as him. Dinner was pretty quiet; if Sue hadn't been there it would have been silent. There would be many more dinners like that.

∽∽∽

Someone was shaking me. I opened my eyes to see Paul standing over me grinning like that freaky Cheshire cat from *Alice in Wonderland*.

'What?' I moaned.

'Let's go for a surf,' he said. 'It's a good morning out there.'

I looked out the window, it was still pretty dark. 'What time is it?'

'Six. C'mon, get up.'

'Yeah, all right.' Paul must have forgotten about the early morning horns us young lads get. 'I'll be up in a tick, piss off.'

I dragged myself out to the back loo. Now there's a good-looking face, I said, inspecting myself in the mirror. My hair, or rather mop as everyone called it, was sitting on one side, giving my head a lop-sided look. There was a bit of stubble back on my chin and a sneaky zit was attempting to pop up on my cheek. It was going to be a beauty.

Paul chucked me a mandarin and we set off for what had become our morning ritual for the last six years.

'Hey, slow down,' Paul said.

'Sorry, I forgot,' I said, handing him a piece of mandarin.

He shook his head. 'I can't eat,' he said.

'Why not?' I mumbled through a mouthful.

'I've got to fast for these tests,' he replied.

I spat a pip, *peeeeooooow* it flew out about two metres.

'What exactly are they doing?'

'Oh, you know, looking at my blood, x-rays all that stuff,' said Paul.

We got to the beach and Paul sat on the sand and lit his rollie. I watched him take that first drag. He coughed a little and held his guts and had a spit.

'Got to give these things up,' he wheezed.

'Yeah, reckon,' I agreed.

Paul stood up and had a stretch. He wasn't tall like me but he was one of those stocky blokes that you know are strong just by looking at them.

'Do us up, will you?' he asked.

As I did I saw the slightest curve in his spine. I ran my finger along his backbone feeling the elevation and decline of these few vertebrae. I felt him flinch but he didn't say a thing. He picked up his old plank and walked into the water. I watched him slide his body onto the board and paddle out. His rollie was still burning on the sand. I stubbed it out and looked up at him, suddenly aware of the effort it had taken him to feign the ease and grace that'd always come so naturally.

The waves weren't that big this morning but they had a beautiful hollow quality that every surfer loves, and to top it off it was only Paul, me and a few seagulls out there.

'I'm on it,' I sang as I spun around and began paddling, feeling the force of the wave and its power looming up behind me. I leapt to my feet and skidded down the face, turning inside the pocket as I crouched down and held onto the rails, the white water spraying everywhere making the *shooosssshhh* sound that makes me feel so happy and free. Man, it was going off. I cracked out a huge re-entry, smacking the lip of the wave. I caught wave after perfect wave like that and as Paul was already out, the choice was all mine. How could he waste such quality? I looked at him sitting on the beach watching me. God, he needed his head read!

By the time I got to school I felt as though I'd already lived out the best part of the day. I knew I was surfing pretty well and I was itching to get back out there and try all those moves again. I must have been in a good mood 'cause when I saw Angie I felt my face break into a big grin.

'Hi,' I said.

'Hi,' she smiled.

'You want to skip first period?' I had an over-whelming desire to be with her again.

'Sure,' she agreed.

We walked hand in hand to the skate ramp. I led her around to the outside of the wall that was hidden from public view. We sat down on the grass together. I put my arm around her and drew her closer to me. I kissed her and she opened her mouth, inviting me to explore its softness.

'You taste of salt,' she said.

'Had a great surf this morning,' I explained.

'Ah, is that why you're in such a good mood?' she teased.

I began to tell her about it but she looked at me in a puzzled way and started to kiss my neck. I guess that was her way of telling me to shut up.

It seemed like no one was interested. I had a bit of a rave to Reece but he always ends up telling you his own stories instead. Harley was in one of his major distracted 'Harley moods' and Toby listened for about three seconds, then changed the subject.

I guess that's the thing about something you do on your own. It's just for you and it's hard to find someone else who wants to know.

When I arrived home from school the house was all dark and locked up – they were probably still at the hospital. To be honest I wasn't really that worried about Paul, he was fit and healthy – he'd put some thirty-year-olds to shame – now someone like that doesn't get sick, I mean bad, serious sick.

It was good having the house to myself. I could raid the fridge, make a big mess, put my dirty shoes on the couch and watch TV without the old girl hassling me.

I'd been chucked out of my room while Aunty Sue was staying. I was sleeping on the fold-out sofa out the back in Paul's workshed. Usually Paul would have moved out there, but Mum and Sue said he wasn't well enough and come to think of it he hadn't insisted like he usually did.

Actually I liked sleeping out there. It was private and got me away from listening to Sue crapping on all the time. I liked the smell in Paul's workshed and the way he always had it so neat and ordered, all his tools hanging in their right place, the machinery sitting along the bench, the fluoros tilted at the right angle, his mask hanging off its hook and the boards he's working on stacked up above. The new blank on the shaping stand was the beginning of my new board. Paul and I were going to design it together up to the last millimetre. I knew exactly what I wanted.

I lay down on the sofa bed, kicked off my shoes and started reading the surfing mag I'd bought on the way home from school. There was an article I was really interested in that was all about getting fit and training specifically for surfing. I'd been thinking about doing some extra stuff to build up my strength and flexibility. Something in my head was telling me if I really was serious about my surfing, now was the time to get it together.

I knew I needed to enter heaps more contests and really get out there. I lay there planning my new fitness regime – I'd go for a run on the soft sand some arvos, start a weight program at the gym and maybe even look into doing yoga. I kind of felt like yoga was a bit of a gay thing to do, but I'd read how good it was for building up strength, increasing flexibility and improving your balance, all of which I could do with.

This thinking was getting me all fired up – I'd go for a run now, start today. It was the 27th of July – that'd give me nearly six months to be in peak condition by the New Year. I locked up the workshed, went inside and changed into shorts and a t-shirt. It was cold, but I planned to be sweating like a pig within a few minutes. I just had to find my running shoes. I looked under my bed – nah, Sue's suitcase was there. I threw everything out of the cupboard – nah, not there either. I chucked out the junk I'd stuffed under my desk nah – I looked at the mess I'd just made and decided to clean it up later before the others got home. Finally I found my runners in the laundry and no wonder, they stank.

I went back to my room and studied myself in the mirror. My arms could do with a pump up, my shoulders were broadening nicely, my lower legs were a bit skinny but my quads looked OK (I'd inherited them from Paul). Not bad, I thought. Definitely room for improvement, but not bad. I jogged down the hall punching the air like Mike Tyson and threw open the front door with gusto. '*Aaagh!*' I yelled.

Standing on the other side of the door were two pale and tired-looking faces. One in sunglasses and one with red swollen eyes. It was Aunty Sue and Mum.

eight

HE smiled at me. I tried to smile back but nerves turned down the corners of my mouth.

'Go get 'em,' he said, squeezing my shoulder.

I looked up at him, my inexperience wanting and needing more.

'You're as good as them, if not better,' he said, then paused. 'Hey, remember, it's meant to be fun.'

I nodded and took a deep breath, knowing these words came from someone who knew. I picked up my board and walked into the water. I was nine years old and this was my first proper surfing contest and somewhere inside I was conscious that he was preparing me for something. I just didn't know what.

~~~

They pushed past me as though I was invisible. I followed them into the kitchen. Sue said, 'I think I'll put the kettle on.'

'Good idea,' Mum replied.

'What a bloody awful day,' said Sue, sitting down next to Mum at the kitchen table.

'The worst,' Mum agreed, burying her head in her hands.

I watched and listened to them, trying to figure out what was going on. They still hadn't acknowledged my presence and it was starting to confuse me.

I now realised Paul hadn't come back with them. I'd thought he was probably bringing things in from the car, but he wasn't. The front door was closed and the kettle had been put on without a mention of his name.

'Where's Paul?' I blurted, hearing a tightness in my voice.

Mum and Sue looked up as if noticing me for the first time.

'Where's Paul?' I repeated.

'Come and sit down, Mitch,' Sue said.

'No,' I snapped. 'I don't want to.'

I struggled to make eye contact with Mum, but she kept staring at her hands.

'Mum, what's happened? Tell me, please.'

'Paul's staying over at the hospital tonight.' Mum reached out her arm towards me. I accepted her invitation and went and sat down on the other side of her.

'He had to have a special biopsy that required him to be sedated,' said Sue. 'So they decided it was best to keep him overnight.'

I looked at Mum. Now I understood why she was avoiding eye contact. She'd been crying – a lot.

Biopsy, sedated? They were the words my mother heard on that TV show and now Sue was using them to describe something in our family.

'So what was the test, what did the doctor say?' I asked impatiently. Why weren't they giving me the info?

'Mitch, it's better if Sue explains,' she sighed. 'She understands all this better than I do.'

I turned to Sue.

'Well?'

'Your grandfather's blood test was abnormal,' she began.

'So?' I prompted.

'So they had to perform what's called a bone marrow biopsy.'

'What's that?'

'It's where they stick a needle, usually into your hip or breastbone, to suck some bone marrow out. Then they examine it to see if it looks abnormal.'

That image made me want to puke.

'Paul hates needles.' I could hear that tightness back in my voice. 'He's completely –'

'They sedated him, darling,' Mum said.

'But what does it mean? Is it bad?'

I couldn't wrap my head around Paul having a needle stuck in his chest. Paul of all people was completely phobic about stuff like that.

'It could be bad,' Sue said, taking me out of my

head and back to earth. 'We won't know until they get the results of the bone marrow biopsy.'

'But bad like how?'

'The doctors think he may –' for a split second she hesitated '– have a type of leukaemia.'

Have you ever had such a blow to the head that you find yourself losing touch with reality for a minute? Voices sounding far away, people moving in slow motion, every feature on their face exaggerated and a feeling that space is closing in on you, competing for your oxygen and your sanity? I think it's called panic, once experienced never forgotten.

We sat around the kitchen table not saying much. Eventually Mum and Sue got up and started doing things around the house. I watched them come and go from the kitchen. I sat there till it got dark. I heard the music for the seven o'clock news on the ABC.

Then I heard Sue shout, 'What have you done, Mitch?' She came storming out of my room.

My room! I completely forgot about the mess I'd made in there earlier. Sue being the big matron was a clean freak and now she was spewing.

'Sorry, I couldn't find my runners,' I explained.

'So you just pulled everything out of the cupboard?' she spat.

'Look, I was going to put it all away,' I said.

'Well do it!' She was screaming now. 'I'm tired and I've had a shitty day. I don't feel like dealing with your mess and slobby habits.'

'Calm down, I said I'd do it.'

'Don't tell me to calm down. Who do you think you are?'

Mum came in. 'What's everyone yelling about?'

'Look at my room, it's a pigsty,' said Sue.

'It's *my* room remember.' I was shouting now.

'Well, while I'm here it's my room and I'd appreciate it if you kept out.'

That really pissed me off, but before I could retaliate Sue added, 'And while your grandfather's sick I'll be staying here and that could be a long time so get used to it.'

'You stupid cow,' I said under my breath. What I really wanted to say was you stupid fat bitch but I knew my life wouldn't be worth living.

'Mitchell,' shouted Mum. 'Apologise to Sue, you can see how upset she is.'

'And I'm not?' I shouted back.

'Just apologise, Mitch,' she said, a bit calmer this time.

'Piss off,' I said. 'Both of you.' I slammed the front door behind me.

I was still in my running gear and it was freezing outside but I couldn't have given a toss. I had to get out of the house and away from that woman. I grabbed my skateboard and headed for the bowl.

'Stupid bitch,' I kept saying over and over again. I was walking fast and my legs felt tight as I strode along the footpath. The icy smoke ejected from my mouth as I puffed and panted each angry word. 'She takes over my room as if she's the boss of the house. The stupid bitch. I hate the way she calls Paul "your grandfather" in that whiny voice. God, Paul better hurry up and get better so she can piss off out of our lives.'

I climbed the stairs of the bowl and walked around the top platform. I stood there balancing my skateboard on the grind pole with one foot, my other foot grounded ready and waiting to drop in.

'Clunk,' came the sound of the wheels hitting the ground as I began to ride down the concrete face.

'Zzrrrrrip, zzrrrrup.' I loved the sound of the wheels running up and down the bowl. Some guys reckon they can't hear that noise while they're skating, but it sings in my ears, soothing like a lullaby.

'Zzzrrriüippp, zzzrrruuuppp, zzzrrriüippp, zzz-rrruuuppp.'

My thoughts unravelled and my anger receded as I lost myself in the mindless task of riding up and down, everything constant, nothing unexpected, or so I thought. I may have been there half an hour before I noticed the figure sitting on the bench watching me. I could tell it was a girl by the way she sat. Although the light of the lamp threw a shadow across her shoulder, I could still make out a shape, which was her pony tail.

I walked towards her, but she didn't move. It wasn't until I stood in front of her that I realised I was staring into the face of Diana Richardson. She didn't say a thing. She looked back at me, those grey eyes empty and cold like the day I'd sat next to her in English. I picked up my skateboard and walked away. Something about her spooked me.

$$\mathcal{SSS}$$

Paul had to stay in hospital a few more days. The results of his tests confirmed he had chronic myeloid leukaemia. I always thought leukaemia was a death sentence, but Mum and Sue told me there were lots of treatments available and that chronic was far better than being diagnosed with acute leukaemia. Anyway, Paul was strong and I knew he could pretty much beat anything.

It was a hassle for me to get into the city to see him, so I spoke to him every night on the telephone. The first night his voice was weird. He sounded tired and sort of far away.

'Hi, Paul,' I said, trying to sound cheerful but probably overdoing it a bit.

'Hey, buddy,' he replied.

'How are you feeling?' A stupid question to ask someone in hospital, especially someone who's just found out they have leukaemia.

'A bit tired, but not too bad,' he replied.

There was a brief silence while I tried to think of something else to say.

'How's your week been?' Paul asked.

'Not too bad,' I said. I didn't know if he knew about the fight with Aunty Sue.

'What's the swell been like?'

'Flat as,' I said. 'I haven't been for a surf since I went with you the other morning.'

'It was pumping then,' he said.

'Sure was,' I agreed. 'You didn't stay in for long.'

'I felt too knocked up, mate,' he sighed. 'What a waste, eh?'

'Don't worry, there'll be plenty more swells like that,' I said.

'So your mum told you the doctors say I have leukaemia?'

It felt surreal him saying those words.

'Yeah, chronic leukaemia.'

'That's right.'

'Chronic's not so bad,' I said.

'Yeah.'

'Apparently there's lots you can do for it. Aunty Sue and Mum were telling me.'

'Mmm.'

'Will you be home for the weekend?'

'Hopefully.'

'Maybe a good swell will welcome you home?'

'Maybe.'

When I got off the phone I felt pretty bad. There was something distant and detached about him. It was a bit like talking to someone I didn't know. The other convos during the week were heaps better, but that first one was the one that stayed in the back of my mind.

I did my usual job at the chemist. Mrs Tran knew all about Paul as she was organising tablets and stuff like that for when he got back from hospital. I had saved nearly three thousand dollars and I had been thinking about buying a car. I needed wheels so I could go and check out the other breaks around the area. At the moment I was dependent on Paul or a couple of lazy mates and it was getting pretty frustrating. I had my L plates as I was already sixteen. Paul and Mum said they were going to teach me how to drive – like I didn't know already?

I was also thinking about using the money to go surfing in Indonesia next year, after my final exams. And then lately I'd been having this major, major fantasy about going around the world on the WQS tour as a trialist. I'd been looking into it on the quiet, but I knew I was going to need a lot more than three grand.

I hadn't had a chance to talk to Paul about it. Him being sick and going to hospital and everything, there just hadn't been the right opportunity. But he'd be home at the end of the week all normal and well again and we could have one of our good yarns. Get a plan into action. Thinking about all that made me realise, even though he'd been gone only five days, I missed our talks in his workshed. You know, a bloke needs another bloke around the house.

Paul was pretty quiet when he got home. He spent the first few days sitting on the couch reading and occasionally going for a wander down to the beach. I don't think he wanted to talk. I don't think he was angry or anything, I just don't think he wanted to talk about 'it', but it was like someone coming home from the barber with a shocking number one and a swastika tattooed on the back and nobody even mentioning it.

I eavesdropped on Mum and Sue one night and they obviously felt the same way.

Sue was doing her usual hassling number. 'He has to talk about it some time. It's not good for him or us. What about Mitch?'

'Look, Sue, he's not ready, that's all,' said Mum. 'He's had – we've all had – a big shock. I mean, let's face it this wasn't meant to be an option.'

'Well, I can't stand the silence.' I heard Sue's voice tremble. 'I can't pretend that this isn't going to happen. You know what I'm like, Liz, I've got to get things in the open.'

'Well, not this time, Suze,' Mum replied quietly. 'We have to respect him over this one.'

'I can't believe you're saying that,' said Sue.

I think the problem with Sue was that she hadn't lived with Paul for a long time. Paul did things in his own time, in his own way. I guess Mum and I were just used to him.

∿∿∿

Jade decided to have everyone over to her place on Friday night – her oldies were in Japan visiting rels. I hadn't seen much of Angie, in fact I'd hardly caught up with anyone since the Paul stuff happened. I was looking forward to a bit of a night sitting around with the boys. Some were going straight from school to Jade's. I decided to go for a run and a surf – my fitness grand plan was in action. By the time I got there the night was well under way and there were heaps more people than I'd expected.

'Hey, Mitch,' Tim screamed. When I walked in he was already legless and red in the face.

I spotted Harley and Reece with a few Year 10 girls, so I went over to say g'day.

'Did you go for a surf?' Reece asked.

'Yeah,' I said.

'Looked pretty fat out there,' said Reece.

'Don't you get cold?' one of the girls asked. Mind you, she was wearing a halter neck top in the middle of winter.

'That's why you wear wetsuits,' Reece groaned.

The girls started giggling. I looked at Harley and moved on. Planet bimbo there.

Jade and Sophie were dancing to one of their mum's old surfing records. Their mum was Japanese and when she'd moved to Australia in the seventies she'd become a full-on surfie chick. Jade grabbed me and tried to get me to dance with her but no thanks! I'm no good at it and it makes me feel like a moron. I tried to escape her grip but she held on tighter. She was spinning us around and around. With a touch of force I could have easily released myself but she would have gone flying through the window.

'Angie's been looking for you,' she sang. She was pissed – really pissed, in fact. It seemed like everyone was.

I found Angie sitting in a group with Jed Travis. They were already talking about the Big Day Out next year.

'You going to come?' Angie asked. 'It'll be sick, everyone's going.'

'Who's playing?' I asked.

Angie and another girl called Tamara rattled off a list of bands like they were reciting history dates. I must admit it sounded pretty good.

'Yeah, I might,' I said.

'Great,' said Angie with a big grin. She gave me one of her looks, got up from the group and walked away. I knew this was my cue to follow. Jade and Sophie were still dancing.

'Angie,' Jade screamed, pulling her away.

They held hands and started spinning each other around and around. They were shrieking and laughing as they went faster and faster. I stood there watching, feeling like a jerk. I spotted Harley alone on the couch so dumped myself next to him.

'Those chicks are smashed,' he said. 'I bet you when they stop spinning around like idiots they'll spew everywhere.'

I started laughing and once I started I couldn't stop. It was like I couldn't find the off switch.

'You right, mate?' Harley said, looking at me like I'd lost the plot and was about to start the three-sixty-degree headspins.

'Ahhh, that's so fucking funny,' I chuckled.

We sat there watching the girls, who were now doing full-on old-fashioned dancing. They looked really unco and kept tripping over each other's feet.

'How's Paul?' asked Harley.

'He's a bit better,' I said. 'He'll be fine in a week or so.'

'I always thought leukaemia was like, you know, bad?' he said.

'Yeah, so did I, but Paul's got the chronic sort. Apparently that's better than the acute type,' I explained. 'So the old girl tells me.'

'Oh,' said Harley.

'And there's lots of treatments and stuff for his one.'

'That's good,' said Harley.

'Yeah lucky, eh?' I answered.

We sat there some more. The girls were now jumping and falling all over each other like they'd created their own mini mosh pit.

'I might slip out the door,' I said.

'Don't blame you,' said Harley. 'I think I'm half a chance with Tamara so I'm gonna stay. See ya, mate.'

I wanted to go home through the park past the skate bowl. Ever since I'd seen her there I'd had this urge to go back. Now I was alone and it was late and dark, something in my head told me she'd be there. So I started walking.

chapter nine

H E took me down to the beach one stormy afternoon when the skies were black and the waves merciless. He sat on the bench, lit his rollie and stared out to sea.

After a long silence he turned and looked at me, his blue eyes pleading for me to remember what he was about to say.

'Mitch, regard the ocean with awe and reverence. It will always be more powerful than you. You just accept with grace and humility what it delivers. Do you understand?'

'Yes, Grandpa,' I replied.

~~~

My feeling was right, she was there. I hid in the bushes and watched her. She was sitting on the railing that ran around the edge of the skate bowl. Her hands were on her head and her legs were raised in front of her, like she was balancing on her bum. I snuck a bit closer and crouched down on the dirt. She swung her legs around and stepped onto the top of the railing, waited for a second then let her hands go and started to walk along the top rail like a tight-rope walker.

After a few steps she'd pause, then take a few more. This went on and on until she'd nearly completed the entire circumference. When she got to the end of the railing, instead of jumping off she slowly raised one leg behind her until it reached the height of her shoulder. She stayed in this position for what felt like ages. I could feel my chest tighten and moisture on my palms, but she looked confident and god she was elegant with her long limbs forming a nearly perfect triangle – but the next thing was what completely blew me away.

'Can you do this, Mitchell?' she said.

I didn't move. I didn't make a sound. I was totally gob-smacked.

'I know you're there,' she said, jumping down to the nice safe ground.

I walked out of my hiding spot feeling a bit like a naughty schoolboy mixed up with a pervert and a peeping Tom.

'How did you know I was there?' I said.

'Don't know,' she said. 'Instinct, I guess.'

Diana went and sat on the bench where she'd watched me just the week before. I sat down on the concrete and faced her. She wasn't pretty, that wasn't the right word.

She was much more than that, maybe striking would be a more accurate description.

'What are you doing down here at night?' I asked.

'I don't know, same thing as you probably,' she replied.

'Isn't it a bit dangerous for girls to be hanging around here at night on their own?'

'What makes you think it's any safer at home?' she said.

'Well, I don't know,' I said, feeling a bit thick. 'Isn't it?'

'Not always,' she answered, getting up and walking back to the railing. 'So can you do this?'

'I doubt it,' I said, following her.

'Come on, have a try.' She climbed onto the top rail. 'You're not scared, are you?'

'Dunno,' I laughed. 'A bit.'

I climbed to the top of the railing and tried to steady myself.

'OK, now start to stand up and slowly let go at the same time.' She demonstrated.

I tried to follow her movements but panicked and jumped down.

'I can't do it,' I laughed.

'Of course you can,' she said, jumping down too.

'Look, you do ballet and stuff. You can do this sort of thing,' I said, trying to justify my inability more to myself than to her.

'But you're a good surfer,' she said, her dark brows crinkling on her face.

'So?' I said.

'So you can stand up on a board in the surf, what's the difference?' she scoffed.

'The difference is if I fall off this railing I'll smash my head open,' I said back.

'Well, if you have that attitude you'll never be truly great at anything.' She looked me right in the face when she said that and I saw her eyes laughing at me, that emptiness gone.

'All right then,' I said climbing back up on the railing. I stood up slowly, trying to think of myself on a wave. I carefully put my foot out and took a step, then another, then another until I'd taken twenty-two in a row. I looked down to see the expression on her face but she wasn't there.

'Hey, Diana?' I called and at that moment lost my balance and fell down with a thud on the concrete. I took the fall on my side. My shoulder and hip hurt, my arm and elbow had a big graze, my cheek already felt swollen and was throbbing badly. I looked around but couldn't see her anywhere.

'Diana?' I muttered.

I lay there for a minute then got up and limped home.

When I woke the next morning I felt like I'd fallen from the top of the Centrepoint Tower. Every way I moved hurt. I went through the night in my head, seeing her or rather her seeing me, talking to her. What was it she'd said about it being no safer at home?

I wondered what she'd meant by that. I replayed the image of her walking along the railing. She seemed to have no fear of falling and hurting herself. I cringed when I thought about how unco I'd been and then to top it off going for a tumble like that.

At least she didn't see, but where had she disappeared to? Now that was weird.

There was a loud bang on the door of Paul's shed.

'Mitch?' It was Mum. 'Mitch, are you awake?' I looked at my watch – it was nearly nine-thirty.

'Yeah, what is it?'

'Telephone.'

'Who is it?'

'Angela.'

God, I'd completely forgotten about her and the party last night. I wondered what she wanted.

When I walked into the kitchen Mum looked at me and shrieked. 'Your face!'

I hadn't looked in the mirror yet to check out my injuries.

'It's nothing,' I said, picking up the phone.

'What's wrong with your face?' Angie asked before I'd even said hello.

'Hey?' I asked.

'I heard your mum say something about your face.'

'It's nothing,' I said. 'I just fell over.'

'When, last night?' Now I was being hassled by Angie. 'Mitch?'

'Yeah, last night,' I answered.

'Well, what happened?' she asked again.

'I fell over at the skate bowl.' I mumbled.

'Oh, is that where you went last night?' she said.

'Yeah.'

'I wondered where you went,' she said. 'I couldn't find you. I thought you might have been like pissed off with me about being drunk and going off with Jade and stuff.'

'Nah.'

'You sure?'

'Yeah, don't worry.'

'Do you want to come over this afternoon? I have to look after my brothers.'

'Um, not sure. I'll see.'

'So, will you ring me?'

'Yep.'

'Sure you're not mad, Mitch?'

'Nah.'

'OK. I'll talk to you later.'

'Yep, bye.'

Mum had the Betadine out and painted me from head to toe. She gave me an ice-pack for my shoulder, which really hurt, and then made me down a couple of aspirin.

'Ah, now you've got two patients,' Paul said, wandering in from the beach still in his wetsuit.

'Have you been for a surf?' I nearly shouted.

For some reason I felt really excited about that prospect.

'Just a quick dip,' he said. 'I think I'll have a nice hot shower.'

'Has Sue given you your needle yet?' Mum asked.

'Needle?' I repeated.

'Yeah, now I've got to have these injections a few times a week,' Paul replied.

'I didn't know that,' I said. 'I thought you were just taking those capsules?'

'Well, the capsules are finished, love,' Mum explained. 'And now these injections have started.'

'How long do you have to have them?' I asked.

I saw Mum and Paul exchange one of their looks.

'Dunno,' Paul mumbled. 'Until I get sick of them.'

'Dad,' whispered Mum.

I watched him shuffle off to the bathroom. Everything seemed to take him a bit more effort these days and I was getting impatient for things to get back to normal. One day at a time, Mum kept saying, which didn't really mean anything to me. I realised I was a bit in the dark about the whole thing. I mean, that was the first I'd heard about him having injections. I decided I'd have to sit down with them and find out exactly what was going on. Then I wouldn't feel like I'm always the last to know, which is usually the way it is. Once I'd come to that conclusion I felt a bit better.

∽∽∽

I completely forgot about ringing Angie. In fact, I forgot that I forgot until she reminded me of course, as most chicks seem to have the habit of doing. I was late to school Monday morning as I'd been for a run then a surf. I was working hard on my backhand turns and things were starting to pay off. It felt good.

Assembly was on in the hall. I snuck in and sat up the back. The captain of the school was giving the standard speech about how great everything was blah, blah. I scanned the rows of students, searching for her long blonde ponytail. I wanted to see her expression when she saw the bruise and grazes on the side of my face. I didn't know if I'd say anything to her, I just wanted her to know that I had tried, even if I did go for a sixer.

When assembly was over I sat there and waited while everyone filed out. I spotted her way back in the crowd.

'Hi, Mitch.' I heard a voice behind me. I turned around to see Angie standing there.

'Oh, g'day,' I said.

'Oh my god, your face is a bit smashed up,' she said.

'Mmm.'

'You forgot to call me yesterday.'

'Huh?' I grunted.

'You said you'd call me and maybe come over,' she said. 'Remember?'

'Huh?' I was still focused on the crowd filing out – I didn't want to miss her.

'Mitch?' Angie said. 'What are you doing?'

'Hey?' I turned around to face her, probably not hiding my irritation very well.

'What are you doing?' I noticed she was blushing. 'Who are you looking for?'

'Oh, sorry,' I said, trying to think what she'd been going on about.

'You haven't heard a word, have you?' She looked hurt and I felt a bit bad.

'Yeah,' I said. 'Um, I'm um sorry I didn't ring you, I forgot. Sorry, Angie. I just have a bit on my mind at the moment.'

'You mean with your grandfather?' she said. 'Jade told me – Harley told her.'

'Yeah,' I said. 'I was going to tell you.'

'That's OK, I under ...'

Angie's words faded into space as I found her face again in the crowd. We looked at each other for a second and I saw the smallest glimpse of a smile light up those grey eyes. For me that was enough. When I returned to earth Angie was still standing there, staring at me like I was really weird.

Who knows, once it may have bothered me, today it didn't. Sometimes when I look back at that day I think of it as the beginning of the strangest times. But when you're actually there in that moment, you don't realise the corner you're turning and perhaps that's just as well. Because maybe you wouldn't turn it, or maybe you'd turn too fast.

chapter ten

I sat on the bench and watched him. After a while he looked up and spoke. 'How was school?'

'All right,' I grunted.

'Give us that sandpaper, will you?' He reached out his hand and I gave it to him. 'You look like you've eaten sour grapes.'

'What?' I muttered.

'Come on, what's up?' he said.

'I dunno.' I paused. 'Everything.'

'Like?'

'Like school, I hate sixth class, I hate the new neighbours and I hate getting home from school later, all that stuff.'

'It's just new stuff, Mitch, you'll get used to it.'

'But I don't want to get used to it.'

'So what are you going to do about it?'

'Dunno,' I answered.

'That's the thing, buddy, there's nothing you can do. You got to learn to take it in your stride and make the best of it,' he said. 'Like surfing yesterday, the conditions were awful, but what'd you do?'

'Nothing,' I said.

'Exactly, you just accepted it and used your skills to work around it and you probably learnt something about surfing in slop like that.'

'S'pose,' I said, feeling a vague sense of relief.

'Change is hard, Mitch, I'm not going to disagree with you there,' he said. 'But there are lots of things in life we can't control and surely as a surfer you understand that, because mother nature's one of our best examples.'

I nodded my head in agreement with his simple explanation.

'And you know what I reckon? Change is the time we learn most about ourselves and our instinct to survive.'

～～～

Mum and Paul were washing up after dinner. Sue had gone home for a few days.

I decided this was the ideal time to have that discussion. I wasn't used to doing things so formally and I knew I was going to feel like a bit of a dickhead saying 'Mum and Paul, we need to talk,' or words like that. But I kind of had the feeling I was going to have to really pin them down.

'Mum, Paul?'

They both turned around to look at me.

'I – um – want to – um – have a proper talk to you guys about what's going on here.'

Maybe there was a flash of panic in their faces but I didn't see it, or maybe I just didn't recognise it.

'Do you mean about Sue living here or Paul not being well?' Mum asked.

'Yeah, all that stuff,' I said. 'I mean, I figured Sue's living here for the moment and all but what I really want to know is what's going on with you?' I gestured at Paul and he nodded his head in a kind of slow uncertain way.

'How about I put the kettle on?' Mum said. 'Who's ready for a cuppa?'

Paul and I sat down on the couch like we were on some American TV show.

'So what do you want to know, son?' he said.

'Well, everything, I s'pose. I mean, I didn't know about you having those injections. And I didn't know you were going to have to go back to the hospital so often for blood tests *and* I heard you and Mum talking about some nurse who has to come in and see you. I mean, what's the story?'

I got that off my chest in one breath.

'He's a bit like Sue, isn't he, Dad?' Mum said, joining us on the couch with a tray of tea and bickies.

'What do you mean by that?' I said. Paul started laughing at me.

'The way you need to know everything,' said

Mum. 'It's good. It's a sign of maturity, don't you think, Dad?' I noticed Mum doing her big hairy glare at Paul, but he was busy staring at his toes like he'd been doing a lot lately.

'So do you have these injections forever?' I asked.

'As long as I feel all right,' he replied.

'And what happens then?' I said.

It was like those words were standing out there on their own, teetering on the edge of a cliff. Everything depended on them and the answer they held. There was silence for a while.

'Paul?' said Mum. 'Are you going to answer that?'

'Well, to tell you the truth I don't really know, Mitch,' he said. 'That's a big question, with lots of things to consider.'

'Like what?' I said.

We both watched him.

'Look, as long as I'm feeling well and can do what I normally do, I'll be happy.'

That was the answer, and it was a pretty typical Paul answer.

'Well, what are your options?' I wanted more from him. 'I mean, Mum, you said yourself when this first happened that there were lots of treatments and stuff available.'

'That's if you want them,' Paul interrupted.

'But if you want to feel well,' I started.

'Look, I'll tell you what's on offer,' Paul said, sounding a bit impatient, I thought. 'Chemotherapy and maybe a bone marrow transplant, that's if I'm not too old.'

Silence from me this time as I tried to swallow those big ugly words.

'God.'

'Yeah, big eh?' said Paul. 'Don't know if I'd be much use after one of those things.'

'Can you surf after a bone marrow transplant?' But Paul was already up and taking the tray back to the kitchen. Mum followed.

I sat there for a while. I think I was trying to imagine what life would be like if Paul had a bone marrow transplant. But I couldn't quite form the images in my mind – they didn't look right.

Mum came out of the kitchen. 'Is there anything else you want to ask, Mitch?'

'Yeah,' Paul called. 'What about asking about your new stick? I got the blank started, you've seen it.'

'I'm stoked.' I had thought it'd be on hold until Paul was completely better.

'Come on out to the shed,' he gestured.

'You mean my bedroom,' I said.

'Yeah,' he laughed.

He put his hand around my neck. His hold was still firm and the familiar feel of his rough fingertips scratching against my skin took me back to where I wanted to be. Away from all those uncertainties.

'Are you sure you can keep doing it?' I asked.

'Well, I've finished my orders,' he said, 'so I'll do

a bit at a time, depending on how I feel each day, I s'pose.'

I didn't sleep in the actual shaping room – you'd suffocate from the dust. I slept in an alcove off the room because that was the only place the couch fitted. Behind that alcove was another shed where Paul glassed and sanded. He still shaped, glassed and sanded most of the boards himself. I think it was probably because he was too much of a perfectionist to pass them on to someone else for fear they wouldn't do as good a job as him, but lately he'd been using a local guy called Luke to finish them off – except for Simon Dobson's, he'd done that stick from beginning to end and it was a beauty. Dobo had taken it to the Gold Coast and I knew Paul'd be anxious to hear how it went. I think that was why so many people wanted Paul to shape their boards. He was always interested in the person's individual ability and what sort of board would suit them best. He didn't just pump out some standard number and he always followed up, no matter if they were a grommet just starting out or an older bloke on a longboard.

'I gather you want something that's smaller and narrower this time? Something that gives you a bit more speed.' Of course Paul knew exactly what I wanted, he always did. 'I think you're ready for that kind of surfing.'

'Yeah,' I answered, feeling completely stoked about it.

'It needs to be slightly concave for speed,' Paul said, running his hands along the bottom of the blank. 'And I think a nice rounded pintail will help you turn smoothly in the hollow pockets.'

He got out the order sheet he'd written up:

Length 6'4"

Width 18½"

Thickness (shaped) 2⅜

Wide point from centre – centre

Nose width 12" back – 11"

Tail width 12" up – 13¾"

Rocker –   nose – 4¾"

                    tail – 2½"

Bottom shape – single into double concave

Rail shape – medium 2¼ low sort

Tail shape – small round square

Fin location – front – 10¾ up

                    rear – 3¼ up

Special shaping – smooth rocker

Special glassing – light

I watched him walk around the blank, viewing it as though it was a rare piece of art.

'And good bottom curves which I'll do myself, by hand of course.' Paul was renowned as one of the few shapers who could achieve an evenly balanced rocker without the help of computerised machines. As a shaper, this was one of his greatest skills – it was a time-consuming task and required real concentration.

'I'll be working on the rocker today,' he'd say to me and Mum and we knew that meant he couldn't be disturbed. Apart from those times, Paul's shaping room was usually a drop-in centre for local surfers who needed a bit of advice on this and that; there was always a beer in the fridge and a story to be told. As a kid when I would get home from school the first thing I'd do is run around to the back shed to check out who was there and what was going on.

'You know, I'm thinking of entering that competition at Kirra next March. What do you reckon?' I asked.

'I hoped you would,' he replied. 'I think you're good enough, that's for sure.'

'It's a tough comp,' I said.

'That's why I'm shaping you this board.'

'I'm definitely going to send in my c.v.,' I added.

'Mitch, no matter what happens, you have to compete, you hear?' he said.

'Yep,' I said.

'Good,' he said. 'That's sorted.'

I felt completely psyched after that conversation with Paul. I surfed every day regardless of the elements, went for a run each arvo after school and then did some weights. Paul was working hard on my board as he wanted me to have heaps of time to try it out in case it wasn't just right. It was good to have him there giving me that extra push when I felt like being slack.

The mornings were still dark and freezing but my seventeenth birthday was only four weeks away and that meant spring and early sunrises. Life was good, I thought, as I wandered down to the beach one morning. You couldn't yet smell the jasmine but you knew it was cooking, almost ready to release its fragrance of happiness and freedom. Not even the chill of the water could disturb my euphoria today.

I was the earliest, the only one out there in the big ocean. I sat on my board and breathed in the peace and stillness. The boys didn't know what they were missing all tucked up in their beds.

'I'm on it,' I whispered to myself as I paddled hard. 'You can't catch me,' I screamed as I tore up the sections. God, it felt good.

The more I got out there the more I learnt about how the wave dictated each move and what it required of me. I was a 'natural' footer and as soon as I'd found the right spot on the board I felt OK. I was learning to surf with the board, using my upper body to follow the board's path and go with its flow, leaning with it and using my arms to support and ground myself.

I knew the right place to start a turn and I knew if I did it at that place it would most likely turn out all right. But that was strategic. What I needed to work on was strength and balance. I couldn't help thinking that if I'd had better balance I wouldn't have fallen off the rail at the skate bowl.

chapter eleven

I showed him my new Grade 6 school photo. He brushed the dust off his hands and took it from me.

'You're still the tallest,' he said, scanning the picture.

'Yeah.'

'Isn't that Andrew Richardson's daughter?' He pointed to the girl standing next to me.

'Yeah, Diana.'

'I should have known,' he said quietly. 'The little girl with the big frown.'

~~~

I was in a car. Paul, Sue and Mum were all driving. I kept saying, 'Be careful in the fog,' and they kept saying, 'What fog? It's clear out there.' We got to this old house and Mum and Sue started covering the outside of it with wallpaper. I walked around the back of the house and saw Diana sitting in the garden.

She handed me these big red flowers. I went inside and telephoned Paul, but I couldn't hear him because he was whispering so softly. Then all of a sudden he appeared in the room and his face was covered in maggots.

I became aware of my consciousness trying to surface, trying to escape the horror and confusion of my dream. I stared at the ceiling, attempting to piece the images together before I lost them completely. I got up and had a piss but couldn't get back to sleep.

I got up again and had a glass of water but still no luck getting to sleep. I lay there feeling very strange, it was almost three a.m. and I had a nagging feeling in the back of my head, like my subconscious was trying to tell me something but I wasn't smart enough to decode the message. As I lay there thinking, the somnolent image of Diana sitting in the grass slid into my consciousness. I got up, got dressed and quietly closed the door to Paul's workshed.

I walked quickly, my arms folded and my head down, trying to fend off the icy wind.

I wished I'd brought my beanie. I heard her before I saw her, or rather I heard her music – competing with the wind – sad piano music filling the skate bowl with an eerie presence. I watched her as she leapt in the air with grace and lightness, hardly making a sound as she landed on the concrete. She danced with precision as though the music guided her every step. I lost all sense of time. It was like I had been hypnotised and it was only her smile that snapped me out of my trance.

'Hi,' she said, slightly out of breath. Her face was flushed and her eyes looked wild.

'G'day,' I replied. 'I couldn't sleep.'

'Me neither,' she said. 'Too much to do.' She turned off the CD player.

'Yeah,' I agreed. 'They're giving us stacks of work.'

'Not that,' she laughed. 'I don't care about that.'

'Well, what do you mean by too much to do?' I asked.

'Just other stuff,' she shrugged.

'Like what?'

She sat down on the ground and started to unlace her ballet shoes.

'You wouldn't be interested,' she said.

'I am interested,' I said. 'Do you want your shoes?'

'Thanks,' she said. I walked over to the bench and got them. She sat there watching me, a smirk just visible on her face.

I watched her feet as she flexed and pointed her bruised and blistered toes.

'Do they hurt?' I asked.

'You get used to it,' she said. 'I soak them in metho to toughen them up but as you can see it doesn't work that well. Are your injuries all better now?'

'Yeah, thanks,' I laughed. 'Although my shoulder's still a bit sore.'

'Does that affect your surfing?'

'A bit.' Those words made something click in my head.

'What?' she said, spotting the flicker of recognition in my eyes.

'I just realised that's probably the other reason I feel so, I don't know, conscious of my balance at the moment.'

'Like how do you mean?'

'Ever since I fell off that railing I've really noticed my upper body and my balance, you know, how I move when I surf.' I paused for a minute. I wanted to explain this properly. 'But it's probably 'cause my shoulder's still a bit sore so when I'm not centred properly on the board, it's like the pain nags at me to fix my position. This all happens in a split second.' I felt like I'd just figured out some incredible maths formula. 'I'm sure that sounds like a load of crap to you.'

'Not at all,' Diana replied. 'My shrink says I'm obsessed with balance.'

'Your shrink?'

'Yeah,' she scoffed. 'The school counsellor told my mother it might help with my – how did he put it – "my withdrawal from people".'

'So what do you do there?'

'He asks me all these boring questions and I answer them, or rather I'm meant to answer them but I don't any more.'

'How come?'

'Because the first time I saw him he said –' she put on a soothing slow voice that'd give anyone the shits after a while – '"Tell me why you think your mother and school counsellor feel you've become withdrawn?" I said, "I'm not withdrawn I just want to focus on one thing only and I don't want any distractions and by the way my mother's a complete piss-head and wouldn't even know what day of the week it was." So you see I gave him the answer then.'

I was shocked but I didn't want her to think of me like that. Like everyone else. We sat there in silence but not an uncomfortable silence. I felt like what she'd told me deserved respect.

'What do you want to focus on?' I asked.

'All I want is to get a scholarship to the London School of Ballet. ASAP and get out of here.'

'Gee,' I said. 'That sounds big. Your sister lives in London, doesn't she?'

'Yeah.' She looked surprised.

'My mum mentioned it once,' I said. 'She cleans your house, my mum that is.'

'Yeah, I know,' laughed Diana. 'She's really nice.'

'Yep, she's good, the old lady,' I agreed.

'I wouldn't call her old, she's just a few years older than my sister.'

'Really?'

'So what else has your mum told you about us?'

'Nothing,' I answered truthfully. 'Oh, she said you had a nice wedding at your place a while back.'

'Yeah, that was an interesting night,' she said. 'Angie Symonds was there helping with the younger kids.'

'Yeah, that's right.'

'She's your girlfriend, isn't she?'

'No,' I said.

'She's not your girlfriend?'

'No, she's not,' I said.

'Oh, I thought you two were going out.'

'No,' I said. 'We're not. I'm not going out with anyone.'

'Me neither and I like it that way.'

'Yeah,' I agreed.

~~~

I came home from the chemist run and went straight to see Paul. He was working on my board like a man possessed.

'Here are your injections.' I handed him the small white box Mrs Tran had given me.

'I don't want anything to do with them,' he said, not even looking up from the blank. 'Give them to Sue. All they do is sting and make me feel shit-house for days and I want to get this stick finished.'

The only time Paul tended to get cranky was when the pressure was on to complete a job.

'The contest isn't till March next year – we got heaps of time,' I said.

'No, we haven't,' he snapped. 'I want you to do a lot of surfing on this.' He thumped the blank, the hollow thud disturbing my feelings of complacency.

'Careful,' I said.

'Sorry,' Paul said. I watched him as he closed his eyes and took a deep breath in and out. 'I want to get it right for you.'

'What's the deal, Paul?' I said. 'Of course you will, you haven't stuffed up a board yet.'

'It's not the board I'm worried about,' he muttered, then cleared his throat. 'I want to take you down the South Coast to Harper's Point to try it on some faster waves like you'll be surfing at Kirra. You need that experience and you need to get a good feel for the board.'

'That'll be sick,' I laughed. Then a thought flashed into my head. 'Do you think you'll be OK to go away?'

'I'm not a bloody cripple, at least not yet,' Paul answered.

'That's not what I meant,' I apologised.

'Yep,' he said. 'I know, I'm just feeling a bit off today.'

I left him alone. I had learnt it was the best way to handle Paul these days.

I went inside the house and gave the injections to Sue. She opened the box and went through it. 'That's strange,' she remarked. 'They've given us a supply for next two weeks. Put them in the fridge will you, Mitch.'

'Paul says they sting,' I said.

'Yep, they're complete buggers,' she replied. 'They sting and then they make you feel like you've got the flu. Fun, eh?'

'He said he wants to take me down the South Coast when the board's finished.'

'That'll be nice,' piped up Mum.

I went and sat on the kitchen bench.

'Here, make yourself useful,' Mum said, handing me a potato peeler.

'Do you reckon he's OK to go away?' I asked.

'Sue's going to shuffle around the injection days so that he'll be well for that weekend.'

Sue came into the kitchen with her diary. It must have been some read, she seemed to have her head permanently stuck in it. I'll bet it didn't have one bloke's phone number in it.

'I'll do the normal days next week,' she said. 'And then the week after I'll do them both at the beginning of the week so he'll be fine for the last weekend in August which is the weekend he's planning to take you.'

'Yes, the 27th and 28th.' Mum looked over Sue's shoulder at her diary and pointed to something. Sue nodded.

'So you two already knew about the weekend?' I said.

Sue snapped the diary shut.

'Well, you know how it is with his treatment,' she said. 'We've got to plan things in advance now.'

'I s'pose,' I said.

Mum began to have a coughing fit. She had her head shoved halfway in the fridge so all you could see was her back jerking up and down.

'You right?' I said giving her a smack on the back. 'Mum?'

But she wasn't coughing she was crying, sobbing actually. I put my arms around her. She felt so small, one squeeze and she'd snap.

'It's OK,' I whispered. 'I know he's getting better. He even wants to go for a surf tomorrow.'

That made her cry even more. I could feel her clinging onto my jumper like it was all she had to hold her up. It made me feel protective and it made me feel scared.

≈≈≈

The next day we did go surfing together, just like old times. Paul woke me up accusing me of being a lazy slob, hassled me to hurry up and get my wetsuit on and then gave me a hard time about walking too slowly. Except this time I could hear his breathing as he pushed himself to keep one step ahead. We sat on the beach and watched the waves. He didn't take a rollie from behind his ear but I saw him raise his hand – a habit from the past – then quickly take it away. The swell was pretty lame but I don't think either of us were really there for that reason – we were just going to get out there and have some fun. We paddled out together and sat out the back watching the colours change in the sky.

'I've been so lucky,' Paul said, leaning over and skimming the water with his hand.

'In what way?' I asked.

'Oh, everything,' he sighed. 'But having my surfing, I've been so lucky to have that.'

'Yeah,' I agreed.

'In some ways I reckon I did my best surfing after your grandma died. If I wasn't looking after Lizzy and Sue, I was in the water. You know, my fingertips were permanently shrivelled,' he chuckled and looked at his hands. 'But that was how I found myself again. I don't know what I would have done if I hadn't had that. Do you know what I'm saying?'

'Yeah,' I answered. 'What do you take me for?'

But he'd already started paddling for a wave. I watched him stand up a little more carefully, but still with such grace. His back was as straight as ever. It looked like he could have been standing at a bus stop casually waiting. He dipped his head into the wave and shook his hair and wiped his nose then stepped forwards and backwards, balancing his weight with precision, one arm out in front guiding the way. He was still a dude.

chapter twelve

I don't know if I was daydreaming, I don't remember much about it except that it was Easter time and the swell had been big all week. I vaguely remember hearing Paul yell and I looked behind at the ocean. It looked like a mountain, with the hugest peak heading towards me — it must have been seven to eight feet. I panicked and frantically started to paddle, but I wasn't ready. I got up but my feet couldn't find the right spot on the board and I fell backwards, my board flipping over behind and hitting me on the head. I was pulled under and my leg-rope snapped as I copped the greatest pounding. I gasped for breath and swallowed water, all the time wondering if I'd ever surface. I could see the light but I couldn't find my way to it.

I felt someone hold me under my arms and drag me out to that light. It was Paul.

'You're OK, buddy,' he said calmly, his grip firm and reassuring, and I knew then I was.

Paul didn't surf again that week; instead he seemed to be obsessed with cleaning out cupboards and drawers. Everywhere I looked there was another box full of papers and other crap. One particular morning I woke earlier than usual and lay in bed listening to a weird shuffling sound. Paul was sitting on the floor sorting through another box.

I sure wasn't going to get out of bed to help – I still had thirty-five minutes left of lie-in before my self-imposed training regime began.

'What are you doing?' I called.

'Oh, sorry mate, I didn't mean to wake you,' Paul replied, flicking through an old mag.

'I thought at first a possum had got in,' I laughed.

'Nah, just me,' he said.

'So what's that stuff you're going through?' I asked, dragging myself out of the cot and putting on my jumper. 'Geez, it's freezing!'

'Is it?' Paul mumbled.

I went and sat next to him on the floor. His face was flushed and his hair looked wet and flat. I reached out and touched his t-shirt, it was saturated.

'You're wet!' I said.

'Yeah, these sweats I get at night, they're really starting to give me the shits. How am I supposed to get a decent night's sleep?'

He didn't look up. He was now sorting through a folder with the precision of a receptionist. I watched him, fascinated and horrified as he flicked the pages, licking his finger between each one.

'You're like a man possessed!' I said.

'Huh?' He finally looked up.

'Nothing,' I said.

He closed the folder and put it into a box marked 'M', which he then slid towards me.

'I want you to have this stuff,' he said. 'It's mostly bits of memorabilia.'

I took out the folder on top.

'Don't go through it now!' he yelled.

'What?'

'Don't go through it now.' His voice fell to a whisper. 'Please.'

'OK!' I said, getting up off the floor. 'I'm going for a surf.'

When I got home after a crap dose of waves Paul and Mum were having some kind of argument. As I hosed down my board outside I heard them yelling at each other. Every now and then they have a shouting match, but this one seemed different – more intense is how I'd describe it.

'Well, we can't walk there. What else was I supposed to do?' Mum yelled.

'But why did you have to ask them?' Paul yelled back. 'Them of all people!'

'She offered, she was trying to be nice,' Mum said.

'I don't want any favours from them,' he growled.

'Do you have to be stubborn about this too?' she snapped.

'Stubborn?' yelled Paul.

'Yeah, stubborn and selfish.'

I heard the kitchen door slam and Mum appeared outside.

'Mitch!' she said. 'I didn't know you were back. Good surf, love? Hungry? Want some breakfast?'

'You all right?' I asked. She seemed pretty stressed these days.

'Yeah,' she said, but I could tell she was trying to breathe deeply to calm herself.

'What were you and Paul arguing about?'

'Nothing much,' she replied.

'Oh c'mon, Mum, it must have been something,' I said. 'I haven't heard you two fight like that for ages.'

Why do they never tell me anything?

'Come inside, love, and have a hot shower,' Mum said. 'I'll make you some porridge.'

I could tell she was doing her usual dodgy number with me but there was something different about that fight and I needed to know what it was.

'I want to know what you guys were fighting about,' I said, wolfing down my porridge. 'And don't say nothing.'

Silence, as predicted.

'Mum, I'm sorry, but it's really starting to irritate me the way you and Paul never tell me anything. It makes me feel like a little kid. Like you reckon I couldn't handle it or something.'

'Age doesn't necessarily mean you can handle something, Mitch,' she said. 'Maturity maybe, but not age.'

'Don't you think I'm mature?' I asked.

'Of course I do. I think you're a wonderful,

wonderful boy. But sometimes knowing things carries certain responsibilities and you don't need all that yet. You have everything ahead of you. If I or Paul for that matter don't tell you things it's because we don't want to burden you with stuff you don't need to know.'

'But how do you know what I do and don't need to know?' I challenged.

'Well, I don't,' she replied. 'I just try and do what I think is best for you.'

'So, come on, what were you two arguing about?' I said.

'The Mazda's broken down,' she began.

'Again?'

'Yes, Mitch, again,' she sighed. 'So I have to borrow a car to take Paul into the clinic.'

'Yeah, so what's the big deal?'

'Mrs Richardson said I can take her car and let's just say Paul's not happy about it.'

'He's always had a thing about the Richardsons. Why?'

'Oh,' said Mum. 'Long story.'

'Come on, you got to tell me now.'

'Andrew Richardson ...'

'That's Diana's father, isn't it?' I asked.

'Yes, and he's actually the same age as your grand-father. Anyway a long, long time ago he took your grandmother out.'

'You're kidding,' I said. 'I never knew that.'

'Well, when your grandmother died he didn't go

to the funeral, he didn't send flowers, he never said anything about it. He acted like it never happened.'

'How come?'

'Because he's a stuck-up dickhead who thinks he's better than everyone else,' Paul said, walking into the kitchen. 'It's bad enough your mother doing the cleaning there, it gives him and his family all the more reason to look down their noses at us.'

'Dad, don't start,' sighed Mum.

'Diana doesn't look down her nose at us,' I said. They both looked at me.

'Don't be too sure of it,' Paul snapped.

'She doesn't! I know she doesn't,' I insisted.

Mum started laughing. 'Hang on, I thought you said she was the biggest loser around.'

'Yeah, well she's not,' I said leaving the table. 'See ya. I'm off to school. You guys sort it out. It's got nothing to do with me.'

It was the first time I'd ever heard real bitterness in Paul's voice and to be honest it shocked me. It felt like I had seen something I wish I hadn't. Maybe that's what Mum was trying to tell me.

When I arrived at school Diana was the first person I saw. She was standing at the gate holding a portable CD player and talking to our year master, Mr Harris. I hung around waiting for her to finish. I felt a bit self-conscious as everyone walked past checking me out, probably dying to know what I was hanging around for.

'Mitch!' It was Harley. 'Are you coming to class?'

'Yeah, in a minute,' I said.

'Did you finish the maths assignment?' he asked.

'Nah, I couldn't …'

Diana had finished her convo and was walking away.

'Hey, Diana?' I called.

She turned around and smiled. I walked up to her and when she noticed Harley following she looked a little panicked.

'You know Harley, don't you?' I really wanted her to feel comfortable.

'Yeah, hi,' she said softly.

'G'day,' replied Harley. 'I'll see you in class, Mitch.'

'Yeah, mate.' I waited for him to walk away. 'What's the CD player for?'

'Mr Harris said I'm allowed to use the junior hall at lunch and in my free periods to practise,' she said. 'He probably thinks that's the least he can do seeing my father paid for the hall to be built. Arsehole.'

'Who, Mr Harris?' I asked.

'No, my father,' Diana replied in a very matter of fact way. 'Anyway, that's where I'll be – got to go.'

'Yeah, bye,' I said.

I stood there and watched her walk away, her feet turned out – Miss Penguin we used to call her in primary. She was different then. I remember her crying a lot and always being in the headmaster's office, but now she gave nothing away.

I couldn't stop thinking about her. All through

class my mind kept wandering to her, her, her. It was driving me mental. Was she in the hall, was she practising, was she in class – was she thinking about me?

I spun one to the teacher so I could get out of class way before the bell went for lunch. I ran to the junior hall to find a group of Year 9s hanging off the window ledges pulling faces at Diana inside.

'Piss off,' I said to them.

'No, you piss off,' some little smart-arse replied.

'Piss off now or I'll shove your head through the window, you little prick.' I stood over him, always a good intimidation tactic. Of course I wouldn't have touched him, fighting's for wankers, but he didn't know that and they bolted. I peered through the window. She was standing on the other side of the room bending forward, one arm stretched out to the side. She was wearing this all-in-one number that showed every curve of her body, I felt my chest tighten. I couldn't breathe or swallow and as I opened the door to the hall I realised my hand was shaking. The same music I heard that night at the skate bowl was playing. I don't know anything about classical music but I understood this music was beautiful and so was she.

I sat on the floor and watched as she turned once, then twice, then three times. I started clapping. I couldn't help it, she was fantastic. She turned the music off and wiped her face with a towel.

'Can I see you tonight?' I whispered.

'Maybe,' she answered.

chapter thirteen

I shouted at him, 'You lied.'

'What?' he said.

'You said you had to be over thirteen to compete at Bells,' I said. 'I found the entry form in your desk.'

'It was only a white lie,' he said.

'Yeah, well what's the difference?' I shouted back.

'A white lie isn't a real lie,' he said. 'It's just something you tell someone or in this case don't tell, when you want to protect them or not upset them.'

'Yeah, well it's a bit late for that,' I spat. 'I know now.'

'But if you hadn't found out —' he started saying.

'But that's not the point, Paul. I have found out and I can't just block it out of my memory,' I said.

'It was my decision,' he said. 'I don't think you're old enough and I don't think you're ready for that level of competition and I don't regret it. But I am very, very sorry you found out because this is exactly how I didn't want you to feel.'

'Too late,' I hissed. 'White lies suck.'

♫♫♫

I set my alarm clock for two a.m. although I didn't get much sleep in between. Two a.m. in the middle of August is freezing, too cold to skateboard. I walked quickly with my head down and the collar of my coat turned up to protect my face from being ripped to shreds by the wind. What was I doing, I thought? I must be losing it being out here in the elements all for the sake of a chick. Yet I knew that was just bloke's talk going on in my head – I longed to see her.

I jumped up and down and did a few push-ups while I waited, I did some sprinting up and down the face of the bowl. Still no show. Where was she? I was sure she'd know this was where I meant to meet. Where else would it be? At two-thirty I wandered through the bush for a while, but that got spooky and there was definitely no sound of her – just a few possums and bats that were starting to freak me out.

I know she'd said 'maybe', but I hoped that was her way of saying 'yes'. At three a.m. I gave up. It was too cold and I wanted to get back to my warm bed. I knew she wasn't going to show.

The weekend was pretty quiet. Saturday night I hung out at Toby's place watching surfing videos. On my way home I went via the skate bowl just in case, but she wasn't there. I even waited for an hour. It was starting to drive me crazy. I was thinking about her all the time. Even out the back with Reece and Toby it was hard to focus on what they were raving about. Only when I paddled for a wave did my mind finally give me some peace. I'd never felt so distracted before. It was weird.

On Monday I got to school early and like a man with a mission went straight to the junior hall but she wasn't there. I looked out for her in class, by the lockers, at lunch time, but she was nowhere. I sat under a tree and ate my sandwiches alone, which was the way I wanted it. I needed to catch up with my thoughts. They were going way too fast – the same way life seemed to be going – and it was spinning me out.

'There you are!' The voice sang but it wasn't the voice I was tuned in to hear. I looked up and saw Angie staring down at me, her eyes wide with the discovery she'd made.

'I've been looking for you,' she said, kneeling down next to me. 'I've missed you.'

I must have looked really stupid but I couldn't think of anything to say. She had disturbed and invaded my reflection. I didn't want to deal with her.

'I haven't seen you for ages,' she said.

I stared at my hands. I found each hair and freckle suddenly fascinating.

'Mitch, are you OK? You seem to be —' Angie stammered for a second, '… I don't know, acting a bit weird lately, not hanging out with us like you usually do?'

Her voice sounded far away, like she was talking to me from the bottom of a hole. Unfortunately she wasn't, she was right in my face. She touched my hair and ran her hand down my neck. I took her hand away and said, 'Don't!'

I got up and walked away.

'Loser,' I heard her hiss.

Wednesday night I sat up with a lump at the back of my throat. I'd been dreaming I was in a box and couldn't get out because Mum and Paul were sitting on the lid. Slowly I felt the lump dissolve and slide down the back of my throat. I got up, put on my coat and trainers and closed the door quietly. From the end of my street I could just hear her music. My feet picked up their pace and I started to run.

When I got there she was walking the rails, a band of some kind holding her wrists firmly behind her back. I watched for a while, scared that any sound would cause her to lose her balance. With her hands still tied behind her back, she lifted one leg in front until it nearly touched her nose. I could hear her counting – 1, 2, 3, 4. Her leg looked so long and straight – 45, 46, 47 – she hadn't even wobbled – 78, 79, 80. I saw a bead of sweat drip from her chin onto her throat – 97, 98, 99, 100. Slowly she lowered her leg, then jumped off the railing. I walked towards her.

'I thought you were there,' she said.

'Really?' I answered.

'I seem to know when people are watching me, even when they're out of my vision. Practice, I suppose?' she said, as though she'd just realised it herself.

'God, I can't believe you kept your leg up for so long *and* while balancing on the railing,' I said. 'That's awesome.'

'Remind me to show you some other balancing tricks some time,' she laughed.

'I should be practising too,' I said. 'I mean I am, I'm surfing heaps, going for runs and doing weights, but man, I could never do that.'

'What's never?' she asked, the blacks of her eyes expanding and constricting. Her eyes could be mesmerising. Sometimes I felt as though I would fall into their grey pool, never to return.

'What's never?' I repeated.

'Yeah,' she teased.

'You know – never,' I answered, a little uncertain.

'There is no never,' she whispered. 'Knowing that gives you freedom.'

'Yeah, right,' I laughed.

'I'm sorry I didn't meet you the other night,' she said. 'It was impossible for me to get away. Some nights my mum gets so pissed she passes out and I have to sit with her in case she drowns in her own spew. It's disgusting.'

'God,' I replied.

'That's as much as an incentive to get to London

as the actual scholarship itself. I'll never have to smell or clean up vomit again.'

'What about your old man?' I asked.

'What about him?' she echoed.

'Doesn't he help you with your mum?' The look she gave me told me this was possibly the stupidest thing I'd ever said. 'No?'

'You're kidding, aren't you?' she scoffed. 'He wouldn't stoop to share his oxygen supply unless there was something in it for him.'

'Oh,' I mumbled, keeping my head down to hide the shock that I knew was plastered all over my face.

We didn't talk for a while. There was nothing I could say back about my family to make her feel like she wasn't on her own.

'Dad hardly comes home anyway,' she finally said.

'Oh?' I replied.

'I was meant to be the child that'd bring them together again, cure their problems. That's why there's such a big gap between my older sister and me.' She shrugged her shoulders and gave me a sort of helpless look, then quickly continued. 'But as you can see, my arrival into the world was truly unsuccessful.' She flung her arms out wide. 'My father drifted completely out of our lives and my mother discovered the joys of alcohol.'

'I don't really know what to say,' I confessed. 'I didn't know any of that.'

'Sorry,' she whispered. 'I'm crapping on, aren't I?'

'No, no, it's cool,' I said, taking her hand and holding it gently. 'I guess I don't realise how lucky I've been.'

Her skin felt soft and her fingers were long and slender.

'But isn't your grandfather sick?' she said quietly.

'Yeah, he has leukaemia.'

'Are you sad?' I felt her fingers curl over mine.

'Yeah, I s'pose,' I answered, feeling a heaviness in my jaw. 'I mean, he's not really the same. He can't surf as much, gets tired easily – you know, hangs out more by the TV and stuff. Things he didn't use to do much.'

'Is he going to die?' she whispered, her hand tightening in mine.

'No, he's going to be OK,' I said. 'He has these injections a few times a week. He hates them. He says they make him feel like shit, but he knows he has to have them, that's the deal. I reckon they've made him a bit weird.'

'Like how?' she asked.

'He goes all manic. Last week he was madly cleaning out his drawers and stuff, but like at all hours of the night and day. This week he's going crazy trying to finish a board for me. It's like he's completely obsessed with it.'

'Maybe he's running out of time?' Diana said.

I looked at her but she didn't return my look.

'For what?' I replied.

'Well, how come he's making you a new board?'

'I'm going in a surfing contest in Queensland in March. He's shaping me a new board for it. We're actually going away this weekend surfing down the coast to try it out.'

'Well, that's why he's in a rush to get it finished,' she said. 'He's not being weird, he sounds really nice.'

'Yeah, he is, he's the best bloke ever,' I said, feeling a bit bad about giving him a sledging before. 'He's also trying to get it finished for my birthday,' I said, feeling a bit stupid.

'When's your birthday?'

'Next week.'

'I mean what day?'

'Wednesday, the first of September.'

'Oh, the first day of Spring,' she cried. 'What a great day for a birthday. I'm on the 23rd of July which is right in the middle of winter. I hate it.'

'Dunno about that,' I laughed. 'The surf's pretty good then.'

'But it's so cold and dark in the mornings,' she moaned. 'I don't get up early to practise on my birthday. It's the one day of the year I let myself off.'

'God,' I said. 'You are focused.'

'I've had to be self-disciplined,' she answered, an edge in her voice. 'I've only ever been able to rely on myself.'

I could never think of anything to say when she said things like that. She seemed so much older than me. I felt naïve and simple when I was with her.

'So, what's it like being seventeen?'

'Same as sixteen,' she replied.

'Great, sounds boring,' I said.

'Mitch, sometimes boring's good.'

I spotted the newspaper van on my way home. I crawled into bed and drifted off to sleep still feeling the warmth of her hand in mine. I felt incredibly happy.

chapter

fourteen

H E gently turned the pages of the photo album as if such care would in turn protect each memory.

'Here's a picture of your gran,' he'd say.

I would study the image of a young woman in a bikini leaning against a longboard and smiling with the energy of life.

But that photo always spooked me. Behind that smile lurked a darkness that would snatch her from the world and the family she loved so much.

He would run his hand along the page as if he could feel her skin and find a sense of what she was to him all these years later. He always closed the album at that page as if afraid of further indulgence and the pain it would mean.

'Turn the page,' I'd say.

'Not today,' he'd reply. 'Maybe another day.'

I understood he lived for the waves and once he had lived for this woman too.

∿∿∿

'Spit it out, Dad, spit it out.'

'Here's the bowl, Dad. There you go, it's OK.'

I followed the voices to the bathroom. Paul was sitting on top of the toilet, a pale blue towel drenched with blood draped over his chest. Mum and Sue were crouched down on either side of him; Mum was holding an orange bowl while Sue held a piece of white cloth to his nose. I looked down at my feet to the blood I had trodden in and smeared on the dusty pink tiles, the grey grout now crimson and stained.

'What's going on?' I heard my voice break.

Paul looked up at me, the blueness of his eyes clouded, his face pale and his look blank. I noticed how small his frame looked even with the bulk of the towel hanging over him.

I felt a rush of panic rise in my throat. I wanted to be sick. He looked awful.

'He's … he's …' I started shouting.

'He's OK,' Sue said gently. 'He's having a bad nose bleed.'

'Do you want me to call an ambulance?' I asked. Isn't that what you're meant to do? Why was everyone so fucking calm?

'No, it's all right. It's nearly over and the clinic doesn't open till eight-thirty. We'll call them then,' Sue replied.

I looked at Mum. She smiled at me but I could tell it was forced.

'It looks worse than it really is, darling,' she said, trying to copy Sue's calmness. I couldn't help but glare at her.

I watched Paul spit more blood into the bowl. It was stringy with saliva and mucus.

'Get us a glass of water will you, Mitch?' asked Sue. I nodded.

I walked out to the kitchen, my mind working like a slide projector flashing images of Paul's face, each more vivid than the last. I couldn't make it stop. I got a glass from the cupboard and stood there staring at the taps on the sink. A distant shattering sound and Sue's voice drew me back to where I was.

'Are you OK?' Sue called.

I looked down at the floor where the cup I had been holding was now in pieces. I crouched down and picked them up. There was no use saving it. I've always thought gluing things back together was stupid.

I handed a new cup of water to Paul. His hand seemed unsteady and Sue reached up and took it.

'Thanks, Mitch,' she said. 'I think we're right now.'

'What's the time, love?' Mum asked me.

'It's five to eight,' I replied, realising I'd only had about three hours sleep.

She stood up and stretched her legs.

'Make us a cup of tea will you?'

'OK,' I said. I glanced at Paul as I walked out of the bathroom and for the first time ever he looked old.

All day at school I wandered around like a moron; trying to keep that image of Paul out of my head was exhausting. When I got home from school I noticed the red light flashing on the answering machine. Usually I wouldn't bother listening to it but a feeling of responsibility and duty was starting to settle heavily on my back. I stared at the flashing light for a while, dreading the news it could deliver. I pressed play and heard Mum's voice. She sounded fine, happy almost.

'Hi, Mitch. It's ten to three and we're still at the hospital. Paul's having a blood and platelet transfusion so we probably won't be home till about six or seven. He's much better.'

I heard a voice mumble something in the background. 'Yep and Paul says don't forget to pick up the train tickets for tomorrow and get your dirty clothes together so I can wash them tonight. That's about it. Oh yeah, we'll bring dinner home and of course don't forget your homework as you'll be away all weekend. See you.'

I had wondered about the weekend. I felt bad thinking like that when I knew the real thing was if Paul was OK. But I couldn't help it, I was really excited about trying out my new stick and showing Paul some of my new moves. To be fair dinkum that was the main thing. I knew I was surfing well. In fact, I was ripping.

$$\mathcal{r}\mathcal{r}\mathcal{r}$$

It was a remarkable recovery. Paul had looked really bad the previous morning but there was no doubt about it, as always he had bounced back to form. Our carriage was starting to empty so we stretched out our legs on the opposite seats and watched the world whiz past, the steady rocking of the train causing us to close our eyes every now and again.

'What time do we get in?' I asked.

'About four-thirty,' replied Paul.

I'd left school at lunchtime so we could get the earlier train and set up camp before it got dark.

'That's a bummer about you not surfing,' I said. 'It'll feel different me being out there on my own.'

'Doctor's orders,' he replied. 'Anyway, I'm here to watch you and see how the board goes. This time I'll be the bloke sitting on the beach all nice and warm stuffing my face with hamburgers.'

I laughed, even though I knew that was little compensation for the man who lived to surf. It also struck me that it'd been a while since I'd actually seen Paul eat a hamburger.

'Hey, it'll be good when you get your appetite

back. You can dig into all those burgers again, yeah?'

He laughed softly. 'Man cannot live on hamburger alone.'

It was an easy walk from the train and down to the campsite, at least easier than I remembered. The last time I was there was when I was thirteen and it was nice to find something that hadn't changed much. Harpers Point, 223 ks down the coast, had always been one of Paul's favourite breaks. It was the ideal spot for a long board as the waves weren't as hollow, but around the corner at the next point was a fast-peeling right-hander fondly known by the locals as 'Balls Break'. And this is what we were here for. By the time we got organised and pitched our tent the sun had gone down. We wandered up town to the local Chinese.

'I love the sweet-and-sour chicken here,' Paul said.

'Yeah, how about some beef in blackbean sauce?' I suggested, scanning the vinyl-covered menu.

'Hey, number one!' A small Chinese man with a big gut came out of the kitchen. Paul stood up and they shook hands like old mates.

'You shrinking,' the man said. 'You no look good.'

'Yeah?' Paul replied, looking a bit embarrassed.

'Me getting bigger you getting smaller,' the man said and patted his gut. 'You getting more ugly me getting more beautiful.' He burst out laughing; it was infectious and Paul and I were soon chuckling too.

'This your grandson?' he said.

'Yeah, remember Mitch?'

'He grown up tall, maybe that why you look like you're shrinking.'

'I wish,' Paul replied. 'Mitch is here to do some surfing.'

'You surf good like number one?' he asked, putting his hand on Paul's shoulder.

'He's better than I ever was,' Paul replied. 'He's going to be great.'

Great? He's going to be great, is that what Paul just said?

'You surfing Harpers Point or Balls Break?'

'The break,' I said.

'You be careful, you may want to have little children some day.' He burst out laughing at his joke, which was the oldest one in the area.

Paul and I discussed our plan for the weekend while I wolfed down the beef in blackbean sauce and the bucket of rice. Paul's plate was untouched.

'Thought you loved the sweet-and-sour chicken?'

'I'm not too hungry,' he said. 'You have it.'

'Ta. I'm still starving.'

∾∾∾

I crawled out of the tent the next morning to find Paul already up watching the sunrise.

'Look how beautiful it is,' he whispered.

Every shade of pink and orange lit the sky with the promise of a great day. But lines of silver and grey cut through these colours, reminding us of the unpredictability of such a promise. Paul had arranged for an old mate to pick us up and drive us to Balls Break. He hadn't left a thing to chance.

'Col's picking us up at seven-thirty so let's go and have a quick coffee,' Paul suggested. 'Did you sleep OK?'

'Pretty good. You?'

'Yep,' he lied.

At least three times I had woken in the night, aware that Paul's sleeping bag was empty.

Col and Paul chatted about old times in the car while I looked out the window recognising bits of scenery along the way. He pulled into the car park and we all went to check out the infamous break. Like Kirra, it was a full-on workout. You can jump in from the point, but paddling back out is virtually impossible because of the channel. So it's a case of getting out, running the length of the beach and taking off back at the point. But I'd been training hard so I was psyched for the challenge and there it was, a right-hander that had such form it went for nearly the entire length of the point. It was about four foot with some five to six foot sections and man, it was beautiful.

Paul and I had a quick chat but I was itching to get out there and try my stuff. The board looked the goods, if that was any indication.

'Let him go,' Col laughed.

Paul looked at me and smiled. 'Go smack 'em.'

There were a couple of guys out there but they seemed pretty cool. Some get a bit aggro about a new face on their turf. I watched for a while then paddled over to the spot where it seemed the best waves were breaking – it sounds so simple but it's an important spot to find, especially if you're competing. I saw my wave coming and started paddling. I felt strong as I jumped up and skidded along the lip, driving the board down the fast-peeling wall, getting barrelled on my first attempt.

'Yahoo,' I screamed as I shot out of the echoing white water.

The entire weekend was like that. It couldn't have been more perfect. Paul and I were stoked and the board felt like it had magical powers. I was doing well, mixing air into the rest of the wave. I had got the furthest out of the water yet, and had managed to land it a couple of times. I was fully amped!

Walking back to the train station I couldn't shut up. All the time Paul was listening and smiling. We got on the train, got settled and I think within seconds I nodded off. It'd been a big physical weekend. I woke up with dribble running down my chin. The scenery changed as we got closer to the city. Paul wasn't next to me so I got up, had a stretch and went for a leak. There was a bloke waiting outside the toilet. I nodded to him and leant against the wall.

'He's been in there for ages,' the bloke said.

'Yeah?' I nodded.

'Don't know what he's doing in there,' he said. 'Longest crap ever.'

'Maybe,' I laughed.

'Hey, mate,' the bloke said, thumping the door. 'This century would be good.'

There was silence.

'Mate, you OK in there?' he said in a kinder tone.

'Yeah, hang on.'

I recognised Paul's voice. I felt something rise in my throat.

'Paul? It's me. Are you OK?'

Silence.

'Paul? Paul!' I rattled the door hard. The latch began to open. I pulled on the door and Paul stumbled out, his head held down, the side of his body hitting against the doorway.

'Paul! Paul, what is it?' I was yelling.

'Come on, mate,' the bloke said. 'Let's get him in here.'

We steered Paul into the carriage. He was a dead weight and it was hard even for the two of us to get him seated. He slumped forward and as I caught him I noticed blood on my hands.

'Paul?' I lifted up his head.

'Paul? Shit!' His right eye was purple and swollen and his nose was bleeding or rather gushing. My head was doing 360s and I frantically tried to remember what Sue and Mum had done the other morning. I ripped off my sloppy joe and with the sleeve held his nose while the bloke ran to get some ice and water. People in the carriage were starting to gather around, some staring, some helping. I wanted to scream, I wanted to cry, I wanted to run away. This wasn't meant to happen.

chapter fifteen

HE sat at the end of my sleeping bag and squeezed my foot.

'You'll be right,' he said, a big grin breaking up the smoothness of his face and making his blue eyes dance in the firelight.

'As you fall asleep, play the moves in your head,' he said, closing his eyes and pausing for a minute as if he himself was waiting in the ocean.

Then he continued, his voice getting louder, 'The paddling for the wave, the turning, the darting in and out of the curl, the speeding up and slowing down. Play it all in your head.'

I snuggled further into my sleeping bag and closed my eyes. I was fourteen and we were camping at Lennox Head for the Grom Fest surfing contest. I had made it to the semi-finals. It was the night before and it was the night he taught me the importance of mental preparation and focus. Tools I would need again in my life.

∿∿∿

Mum, Sue and I waited in casualty while they took Paul for a head scan. The doctors thought he had probably collapsed in the toilet and hit the side of his face. But they wanted to check he hadn't hit his skull because they were worried he may be haemorrhaging or something. I felt pretty upset. No, that's a lie. I felt totally ripped apart inside, like I'd been given the biggest hammering ever.

Mum and Sue kept saying how well I'd done and how lucky Paul was to have me there but I was pissed off for falling asleep. If I'd stayed awake at least I would have wondered where Paul was. I would have eventually gone looking for him and maybe I could have got to him sooner. But now everything was fucked up thanks to me for wanting to try out the board at some stupid place. I should have known Paul wasn't up to it – I should have known, I should have fucking known.

They wheeled Paul in after the scan and he seemed a bit brighter.

'The doctor said he'll come and see us in about half an hour,' he said.

'Who feels like a coffee?' Sue said.

'I'll go and get them,' I offered. I felt like slipping away into the darkness.

'You want me to come with you?' asked Sue.

'I'll be right.'

I took Mum and Sue's orders and went in search of the cafeteria.

As soon as I hit the outside I realised how badly I needed some fresh air, how stuffy and cramped it was around Paul's bed with the curtains closed and no windows open.

I thought about people who were claustrophobic and wondered how they handled feeling trapped all the time.

I found the cafeteria, flicked through some mags, ordered the cappuccinos and took them back up to the casualty building.

The curtains were still closed around the bed and it was hard trying to open them with a hot coffee in each hand. As I fumbled around I realised the doctor was in there with them. I recognised his deep voice.

'But this is what's going to happen,' he said. 'More and more as the disease accelerates. It's only going to get worse.'

'But what about if we continued?' I heard Sue say.

I heard Paul whisper something in reply. I think he said, 'I told you no. We agreed to that months ago.'

At that moment I blundered in with the coffees. Everyone turned and looked at me.

'What?' I said.

'Dr Mellish, this is my grandson Mitch.' Paul sounded serious.

'Hello,' I nodded. I'd seen him before but had never had the royal intro.

'Nice to meet you,' he said, his eyes fixed on me. He smiled at me like I was a young boy. That smile stuck in my head and it took me a while to work out why.

By the time we got home it was late. Paul had to stay at the hospital. It was depressing seeing him wheeled away to his ward. None of us felt like talking. I gazed out the car window and listened to the radio, one song blurring into the next. My mind was numb.

I didn't even feel like a surf the next morning. This was a Monday I hated. Everything was a bit of an E for effort. I hung out at school on my own, somehow finding my way to each class. Everyone looked like they were rushing around but I felt as though my legs were dragging behind me.

After school I went and sat in the junior hall. I didn't know if she was going to turn up but I didn't know where else to find her at that time of day. My eyes felt heavy.

I was so tired I wanted to lie down and sleep forever.

When I woke up she was sitting next to me stroking my hair. It was dark and I was shivering.

'What time is it?' I asked, feeling disorientated.

'It's nearly six,' Diana replied.

'How long have you been here?'

'About an hour.'

'And I was asleep all that time?'

'I know about your grandfather,' she said. 'Your mum rang this morning.'

'God, it was bad,' I uttered. 'I was shit scared. You know I thought he was going to – you know – die and I didn't want to be there. I don't know where I wanted to be but I didn't want to be there. You know what I mean?'

'Of course I do,' she said in a soothing voice, all the time stroking my hair with the softest touch. I closed my eyes and nearly heard my body sigh with relief.

~~~

Tuesday arvo Harley was waiting by my locker.

'You walking home?' he asked.

'Yep,' I replied.

We swung our bags over our shoulders and walked out of the school, dodging our way through kids queuing for buses, kids yelling at each other and throwing hats around. Two Year 7 boys were having a fight and rolling around on the footpath, ignoring the teacher's yells. Sometimes it's like being in the nut house.

'Did you tell Angie to piss off the other day?' asked Harley.

'She was in my face,' I moaned.

'Tell us about it,' Harley said. 'I know what she can be like – remember, I went out with her too.'

'I wasn't like going out with her.'

'Well, she thinks you were.'

'Is that what she said?'

'Yep and she's real dirty with you now.'

'You're kidding!'

'I thought I better tell you she's going on about you and Diana Richardson. She's telling everyone how you're hanging down at the junior hall at lunch and stuff with her.'

'She's a desperate.'

'You said it, buddy. Guess who she was hanging off the other night?'

'Dunno, who?'

'Jed.'

'And she called me a loser.'

'Anyway, just be cool, Mitch.'

'Hey?'

'Look, you always are, mate, but I know things aren't going too well with Paul and stuff. I know you think I got my head up my arse most of the time, but you're my best mate and I feel like you're drifting a bit. You know what I'm saying?'

'Yeah. Thanks, mate.'

'No worries, brother.'

'Got to go. I got the chemist run to do.'

'Yep. See you round.'

When I arrived at the chemist, Mrs Tran was packing Paul's injections into a box.

'Are they for me to take home?' I asked.

She looked at me in a puzzled sort of way. 'No, I'm sending them back.'

'Where? To the hospital?'

'Yes, that's where they came from,' Mrs Tran answered, again giving me that funny look.

I picked up the chemist bag. 'Just the usual deliveries?'

'Yes, but can you do the Mayers last. They have the community nurse there this afternoon. Mr Mayer is very bad now.'

When I knocked on the door of the Mayers I had already decided it was going to be a speedy visit. Something that Mrs Tran had said was starting to puzzle me and I wanted to get back to the chemist and get home.

'Hello, Mitch,' Mrs Mayer said, opening the door to their dark and dingy home. 'The nurse has just left and I forgot to ask her to label these bottles for me. My eyes are so poor these days even with my glasses. Could you do it for me, love?'

'Sure.'

I followed her down the hallway and before I could think about where she was leading me I found myself face to face with Mr Mayer.

I wasn't prepared. He was skeletal. Every bone in his face protruded but the rest of him was sunken and hollow looking. His eyes weren't closed properly so the whites were just visible.

He had an oxygen mask over his mouth and nose

which fogged up every now and then with his breathing, which I could only describe as shallow, laboured and erratic.

I stood there staring. I wanted to look away but I couldn't. I was frozen and the walls were starting to cave in. Mrs Mayer was saying something and passing me a bottle.

'I can't,' is what I think I said. I don't remember. I just remember running down the hall and out of the house. There was something at home I had to find.

∿∿∿

I ran into my bedroom, which was cluttered with Sue's stuff. I went through her suitcase and searched through my drawers, which were filled with her clothes. I pulled out each drawer and emptied the contents on the floor – bras, undies, belts, a scarf, some t-shirts – it wasn't there. I crawled into the cupboard, chucking out shoes and bags.

I looked under the bed. I was sweating and panting, my hands shaking, my legs like mush. I heard the front door and went stumbling out.

'Where is it,' I roared. 'Where the fuck is it?'

Mum and Sue stood there staring. I ran at Sue. Mum screamed.

'Give it to me,' I shouted. I pushed her but her sturdy frame supported her and she grabbed my hands.

'Mitch! Mitch, what is it?'

I was throwing myself around the room like a poisoned animal, jerking and kicking at anything in my way.

'Stop it, Mitch, stop it!' Mum was sobbing. 'Tell us what it is? You're scaring me.'

I composed myself long enough to say, 'I – want – to – see – Sue's – diary.'

Silence. Earth-shattering silence.

'Mitch, Mitch,' Mum started saying. 'Darling, you –'

'No, Liz. He knows.'

Sue got her diary and I snatched it from her.

'I'm so sorry,' she whispered.

'Fuck you, fuck the lot of you.'

sixteen

I cornered him. 'Why will you never tell me anything about him?'

'Because he's a loser,' Paul replied.

'You always say that, but why? Why is he a loser?'

'Well, for a start he pissed off when he found out your mother was pregnant with you.'

'Yeah, I know that but what else?'

'He didn't get to watch you grow up,' he said. 'He lost out big time there.'

'You always say the same thing, Paul.'

'Because that's all I want to say about him.'

'But you can't just decide not to tell me. I have every right to ask about him.'

'It's the way I do things, Mitch. I tell you what's going to make you feel good, not what's going to make you feel bad, especially when there's no point.'

'Look, I don't want to find him or anything. I'm just curious, that's all.'

'Well, don't be. He's not worth it. Trust me on this one.'

What was it that Paul once said about white lies? They're something you tell someone when you want to protect and not hurt them. Well, there it was on a page dated the 23rd of August in Sue's handwriting: 'Paul to stop all treatment.' Five words. That's all it took to surrender your life. But why, why was he giving up? Wasn't there so much to live for? Didn't they say 'chronic' was the good leukaemia, the one that had plenty of treatments and maybe even a cure? And why didn't they tell me? Why did they let me believe there was hope? Sucker, sucker, I'm a fucking sucker – they were probably never going to tell me. I felt sick. I wanted to throw up all the disgust I felt inside, purge myself of all their deceit and lies and slam my head against the wall over and over again for being so stupid. So gullible, so trusting.

There was a pathetic little knock on the door. It was Sue.

'Mitch, please. Please let me explain.' She was walking towards me.

'Don't come near me, don't come fucking near me,' I hissed.

'Mitch, it was so important to Paul that he was well for your birthday, he … he really …'

I jumped off my bed and started pacing around the room. I wanted to grab something, I wanted to smash something and feel the pieces shatter in my hand.

'Since when have birthdays been such a big deal in this house?' I shouted. 'That's the biggest load of crap I've ever heard but I guess you think I'm so dumb I'd swallow anything.'

'Mitch, this was Paul's decision. We had no say in it, please believe me.'

'I'll never believe another thing you say – or rather don't say, that's what you all seem to be so good at.'

'Mitch,' Sue was pleading now. 'Mitch, all Paul could focus on was shaping you that board, taking you down the coast and preparing you for –'

'For what? His death? Or was that just going to be some kind of minor event?'

'For Kirra, for your future,' cried Sue.

'Fuck Kirra and fuck my future. What hope do I have when I'm surrounded by liars? And fuck my board.' That was hard to say or maybe I mean hard to believe, but it was ruined now. All my dreams felt as though they'd been poisoned. All that time wasted.

From the window I could see my new board. The black and green pattern that I had helped design suddenly seemed like a very sick joke. I pushed past Sue and went outside to where it was lying on the grass. I ran my hand along the still smooth fibreglass surface and saw his signature underneath. It read: 'For Mitch, forever, Paul.' I picked it up and smashed it against the frangipani tree. Once, twice, three times. White milky sap started to ooze from the branches as I hit it over and over again.

Mum and Sue came running out, screaming at me to stop, but it was only when the branch had snapped and I had nothing left to whack that I could stop. I stared at the tree, the frangipani tree with its magic sweet-smelling flowers. What a load of bullshit. I dropped the board and walked out the gate, making sure I didn't look back at the destruction I had left behind.

~~~

I walked and walked. I didn't know where I was going but that didn't matter. I just needed space. I saw people wheeling trolleys out of the supermarket and Trevor standing outside his milkbar chatting, people walking home from work carrying their briefcases and a couple walking their dog. Why was everyone acting like nothing had happened? Didn't they realise how fucking angry and bad I felt? It was seven p.m. and the lights inside the houses started coming on as families sat down to dinner together as we once had. But now it was different and I felt sure it could never be the same again.

I climbed to the top of the headland and sat there staring at a sea that looked like folds of black velvet.

The Southern Cross was clear and strong. I tried to draw some strength from its order but it was no use. Nothing was going to take the pain away – nothing. I lay down and closed my eyes, willing the night to swallow me up. I think I slept. I had all these weird thoughts that I seemed to lose every time my consciousness surfaced. It was just before eleven-thirty when I finally sat up, feeling disorientated and pissed off that I was still there and still me. Thirty-five minutes till my seventeenth birthday and there was nothing to celebrate.

I started to walk further up the headland. Was it between the third and fourth or the fourth and fifth Norfolk pine that the Richardson mansion stood facing out to the sea? It was strange, but as I got closer to her house I started to feel less alone. It didn't matter that she had no idea where I was, I knew that somewhere in that house she was either sleeping or practising or something like that and it made me feel connected to her.

I crossed the perfectly manicured lawns and saw the navy-blue four-wheel drive parked outside the garage. I was about to step onto the driveway when I hesitated, took off my shoes and quietly crept across the pebbles, a smirk on my face for being so clever. I had been to the house just once before with Mum and I remembered she'd entered through a side door to the kitchen. The handle turned smoothly and there I was standing in their kitchen, which was about twice the size of our whole house. I snooped around until I came to the stairs and it was only then that I felt my heart thumping on the side of my chest. A brief feeling of doubt crossed my mind. Should I be doing this? What happens if I get caught?

At the top of the stairs I heard the music, the music that had always been my direction to her. I took a deep breath and steadied my hand on the door and with a gentle push I entered her world.

'Hello,' she whispered.

It caught me off guard seeing her sitting there calmly as though she'd been expecting me. But then another part of me wasn't. It was like I knew this was always going to happen.

'Are you OK?' she asked.

'Yeah. I mean no, no I'm not. That's why I wanted to find you.' I sat down on the bed next to her. 'They've been lying to me.'

'Who?'

'All of them. Mum, Aunty Sue, Paul, probably others.'

'What about?'

'Paul's dying and they've known all along.'

'Oh, Mitch,' she sighed, running her hand across my face. 'That's so awful.'

'Here am I like some dumb dickhead thinking he's having treatment and like everything's going to be OK and it's not. He's not. He doesn't want any more treatment. He wants to die and he just fucking lied about it. Can you believe it?'

'Adults can be so fucked,' she said.

'But, but … Paul?' I said. 'It's like everything I've worked towards is pointless is, is …'

'Mitch, you have to be strong. You can't let them get to you.'

'But why? Why is he doing this?'

'You can't think about that. You have to think of yourself, protect yourself and stay focused, really focused so that nothing can get in your way. You can't just let everything fall apart because of what they've done to you. You have to fight back for yourself and only for yourself.'

We lay on the bed staring at each other. We hadn't even kissed but the closeness I had with her was like nothing I'd ever felt before. It was complete. I cannot describe it in any other way.

'You know that music I was playing?' she said.

'Yeah, what is it?'

'It's by Grieg. It's the second movement of his piano concerto in A minor.'

'His what in what?' I laughed.

'But do you know why I play it?'

I shook my head.

'Because it gives me hope. It inspires me.' She got up and turned the music back on.

'Listen,' she whispered. 'Listen how he takes you through the pain and just when you think it's unbearable he shows you triumph on the other side. That can be you.'

For someone who's never listened to classical music I lay there feeling a little weird but I trusted her. I wanted to know if I could hear what she heard.

'Close your eyes,' she said.

We lay there together, our arms wrapped around one another and listened.

'It starts with the strings,' she whispered. 'You know the violins and stuff.'

After a while she said, 'Wait, listen to this.'

Gently the sound of a piano rolled in. I felt her shudder. Gradually the music became louder and wild like something bad was going to happen. Then I heard it, the triumph. It was like getting to the top of a mountain and shouting out to the world, 'Hey, look at me. Look what I did!' I felt this overwhelming feeling of happiness and strength.

'Wow,' I said.

She looked at me and she was crying. 'Why does it have to be so hard?'

'I don't know,' I replied.

chapter seventeen

I heard myself groan as he helped me stand up. 'Decided to have a nap in the garden, eh?' he laughed, brushing the dirt off me.

'It's not funny,' I moaned.

I looked down at the dinner jacket I'd hired for the Year 10 formal. It was all splattered in yellowy brown mush.

'I feel shit-house.'

'The sponsors will be here in an hour,' Paul reminded me. 'They'll love the one eyebrow.'

'Oh no, no,' I cried, reaching my hand up to my face.

'We better get you cleaned up. By the way, was it a good night?'

'I can't remember,' I groaned. 'I think I'm going to throw up again.'

Paul came home from hospital a week after my birth-day. I had managed to dodge visiting him by saying things like I had assignments, work, anything I could think of to avoid looking into those eyes. I spent most nights at Diana's after her mother had crashed out, which could be as early as six or seven. Diana wasn't exaggerating when she called her a drunk. I had never seen anything like it. Diana would show me the empty bottles of vodka and gin she'd clean out of her mother's drawers, and that was on top of the ones she'd put out in public view in the recycling box.

It felt strange staying in a girl's house yet never meeting or talking to any parents. Her mother was always crashed out in bed with the door closed. And she was right about her father, he never came home. We had this huge house to ourselves yet we always hung out in her bedroom. It had become our refuge from a world that had let us down.

The time I spent at school or at home was like killing time while I waited to go back to the safety of her room and the comfort of her. But somewhere, deep inside, I wondered how long I could go on like this.

I think it was after about my eleventh night there that I got home early in the morning to find Paul sitting on my bed.

'Are you going for a surf?' he asked. 'Or have you given up on that too?'

I looked at him and he stared right back. Even

though he sat there shrunken and frail, I could tell he was still a strong man.

'Hey?' he said. 'What are you trying to do to your mother? What's the story, mate?'

'You tell me.'

'OK,' he replied, standing up and walking over to me. His steps were small but he still stood with that straight back. 'You're really angry with me so you've decided to just chuck it in, give up completely.'

'And you haven't?' I replied.

'We're talking about you, Mitchell. You have your life ahead of you. Everything's there waiting for you.'

'You reckon?' I mocked. 'You don't know how I feel. You don't, you don't know shit. So don't even make out like you understand.'

'Is that why you're going to her place, because she understands?'

Those words made me flinch.

'She knows what it's like to live a lie.' I wanted those words to shock every nerve in his body.

'I'm sorry you feel like that,' he said. 'But be careful.'

'Of who?' I snapped.

'Yourself,' he paused. 'And maybe her.'

'You don't know anything about her.'

'I know she's an angry girl and maybe she has every right to be. She's been hurt, let down, neglected, abused, whatever you want to call it. But you haven't. You've been loved and encouraged all your life.'

'So what are you saying, that because I've been loved and encouraged it's OK to spin me the biggest stories and make out you're doing something when you're not?'

'You're still angry,' said Paul. 'There's no point talking to you now.'

And he got up and left. For a second I felt like chasing him, slamming him up against the wall and saying, 'Don't fucking walk away from me, you prick,' but he was almost a shadow.

ฌฌฌ

I started surfing again in the mornings. Sometimes it felt good, often it didn't. I was tired all the time and it was hard to focus on anything. I felt like my centre of gravity had shifted and I had lost my balance. I didn't want to surf with my new stick. I didn't even want to look at it. It had suffered a bit of a ding, but it had come off way better than the tree. I hadn't realised how soft those franigpanis are. Paul had repaired the board and the tree. One arvo I'd got home from school to find Mum, Sue and Paul kneeling around the remains of the frangipani tying the stump to a stake. Mum and Paul had looked up at me for a second, enough to make me feel like a dickhead. I didn't care, it was only a tree. It was Sue who came over to me.

'It's OK. They'll be able to fix it.'

'Lucky tree,' I'd said and walked off.

One night as I lay there next to Diana I tried to imagine being at Kirra and paddling for its perfect wave. It was fast and hollow like the ultimate Kirra sand barrel, but I couldn't get on it. Even in my mind I was unable to balance my weight over the board and find the right spot for my feet.

'I've lost it,' I whispered to myself.

'Lost what?'

I'd thought Diana was asleep.

She said it again. 'Lost what?'

'I don't know. My balance, my focus. It's just gone.'

She jumped out of bed and started getting dressed.

'Get up,' she said.

'What?'

'Get up.'

'It's the middle of the night.'

'So? That's never stopped you before.'

I started getting dressed too. 'Where are we going?'

'You'll see.'

I followed her through the garden out onto the cliff. Her long legs flew behind her as she ran down the headland.

'Wait,' I called as I tried to keep up with her.

It's not that I'm a slow runner, it's that she seemed to know exactly where she was going and I didn't. She bolted through the bush dodging logs and rocks, weaving in and out of the scrub like she knew the track by heart, especially in the black of the night. She didn't stop until she reached the edge of the cliff and there was nowhere else to go.

The moon was full that night and cast its glow over the sea and onto the place where we stood. Her face was flushed and she was breathing hard, her hair tangled around her face and neck. With both hands I freed the hair from her face and looked closely at her.

'What are we doing here?' Her eyes looked wild with terror. I felt like they were desperate to tell me something. 'What is it, Diana?'

She buried her head in the curve of my shoulder. The hairs on my neck tingled as I felt her hot breath on my skin. I stroked her hair and kissed her head, smelling the sweet scent that would always remind me of her.

'I've never told anyone this,' she whispered. 'This has always been my secret.'

I stood there holding her, waiting until she had found the courage to tell me what no one else had heard.

'When I lose my focus and my sense of who I am or rather who I want to be, I … I challenge myself. I push myself to see how far I can go. To see if I'm good enough. Do you understand what I'm saying?'

'Sort of,' I said, although I think I didn't really have a clue.

'When you said you felt like you'd lost your sense of balance I understood what you meant. Balance in every way is everything to me. Without it I can't dance and that means I can't escape.'

'Escape from what?'

'Everything. My life, my parents, myself – not you,' she smiled. 'You don't make me feel like that.'

I looked at her. She made me think of a spider trying to find a way out of its web.

'I still don't get why we're here?'

'Do you remember once I told you I'd show you some of my other balancing tricks.'

I remembered her saying that. Those nights at the skate bowl seemed a long time ago.

She looked nervous and uncertain. 'Promise to keep this a secret?'

'OK,' I said.

Diana walked to the edge of the cliff. I mean the very, very edge of the cliff.

'What are you doing?' I shouted. I moved closer to her.

'Don't,' she said firmly.

She was facing the ocean. I could see half her shoe was edged over the cliff.

'Diana,' I said. 'Come on, come back, you're freaking me out.'

She stood there as still as anything then slowly raised her leg behind her. She wobbled for a second then I heard her take a breath. My heart was thumping about a thousand beats a minute and throwing up was not completely out of the question.

'That's enough,' I said. She ignored me. 'Stop it, Diana.'

Gracefully and slowly she lowered her leg and walked away from the cliff's edge.

'That's how I find my focus,' she said. 'How about you? How are you going to get yours back?'

'No way am I doing that. You could slip, fall anything. I mean, how do you know if your –'

'I don't,' she interrupted. 'All I know is that without my strength I've got nothing.'

The little girl with the frown is how Paul used to refer to her and there she was looking at me like that. I think it was only then that I started to understand how complicated her life had been and how simple mine was. But like many revelations, they take a while to surface.

chapter eighteen

I passed him an ice-cream. 'I got you hokey-pokey.'
'Ta,' he said, taking a big lick.

The swell was dead but there were other things to look at like a group of teenage girls rubbing suntan oil into their legs. I watched the curves and limbs move around on their towels. I looked at Paul and he winked.

'Keep it in your daks,' he laughed. 'You're just window shopping.'

'You right?' I said.

'Well, it's like fifty different flavours to tempt you,' he said. 'All different and all good but only one will be for you and you'll know it a mile off.'

'Yeah, thanks for the tip, mate,' I said, rolling my eyes at him. 'I noticed you picked hokey-pokey.'

~~~

Paul was in and out of hospital over the next month. Sue had convinced him to have blood transfusions when he needed them. It seemed to make him better for a few days, which is probably why he agreed to it – he could actually have a life. The rest of the time he just lay around looking pretty bad and those were the times I didn't want to know about him. Some days I felt such intense anger towards him it occupied every part of my body. Those were the days I didn't trust myself even to look at him.

Diana was getting ready for her big scholarship exam and was practising nearly all the time in the junior hall, at home or at her teacher's studio. I've got to say her focus and commitment were inspiring. We didn't talk about what'd happen if she won the scholarship and went to London. I think it was easier for both of us to pretend it wasn't really happening because the thing was if she did get it she'd be gone before Christmas and that wasn't too far away.

And what was I doing with myself? Sweet FA – going to school, surfing, hanging out with Diana, hanging out a bit with Harley and doing my best to avoid everyone else. I felt agitated nearly all the time. It was this continual feeling of wanting to give something or someone a big whack.

～～～

It was in the week before Diana's exam. I remember it was a Thursday because I was going to play touch footy that arvo. I actually felt pretty good that morning. I'd been for a surf and when I walked to school I got a slight whiff of summer coming. The vines of jasmine that climbed on most of the fences around here were starting to flower and for me that's always been a sign of happy times.

At lunch I went to see Diana in the hall. She looked like she was kind of head-butting the wall and was making this weird low groaning noise.

'What are you doing?'

She spun around to face me. 'Someone's stolen my CD player.'

'You're kidding?'

'And my CDs – all the music I need to practise.'

'Did you see anyone hanging around?'

'That mate of yours, Tim.'

'Tim? Are you sure?'

'Of course I am,' she snapped. 'He hangs around here a lot watching me with this … this revolting smirk on his face. The pervert. He's always given me the creeps.'

'Tim? Why didn't you tell me?'

'Well, what would you have done?'

'Smashed his head in.' And I meant it too. It even felt good saying it.

'He's your friend, Mitch.'

'Not if he's doing that to you. You should have told me.'

'I don't know,' she mumbled. I watched her crack the knuckles on her hand. 'I mean, I don't think you really want to advertise the fact that you and me are like …'

'Together?' I said.

'Yeah,' she replied, her forehead breaking into a frown that made her expression look awkward and unsure.

'Diana,' I said. 'I'd do anything for you.'

Her head was hung low. I had to lift it gently so that I could see her eyes. She could try and hide her feelings with silence but she couldn't hide those eyes.

'OK?' I whispered my lips brushing against hers.

When I left the hall I could feel an energy rising in my body. I knew even then it wasn't a good energy but I didn't care. I found Tim sitting on the grass with some Year 10 girls. He looked up at me and grinned like some real smart-arse.

'Get up,' I said.

'Huh?' The grin dissolved.

'Get up,' I said, a bit louder this time.

'What's your problem?' he replied.

'I said *get up*.' And as I shouted I grabbed him by the collar and pulled him to his feet. One of the girls screamed.

'What the fuck are you doing?' he yelled, struggling under my grip.

He was a big guy but I was fit and I wanted him badly. I dragged him over the grass. He was arms and legs everywhere trying to break free. But he couldn't and the more pathetic he looked the stronger I felt. I pushed him up against the wall and held his jaw, pushing the bones until I was sure it hurt.

'Where is it?' I growled.

'Where's what?'

His eyes looked frightened but I felt no mercy. A crowd was gathering around but no one tried to stop me.

'I know you've got her CD player.' I felt the saliva frothing in my mouth. 'She told me how you perve at her, you disgusting pig.'

'I don't have it,' he yelled. I pushed him against the wall. He hit his head and cried out in pain. 'I don't, I promise.'

I felt a hand on my shoulder.

'Mitch!' I recognised Harley's voice. 'Come on, mate.'

'He's nicked her CD player, Harley!' I couldn't stop my voice from shaking. 'He's watching her. He's a fucking pervert.'

'Yeah, mate,' Harley said calmly. 'Come on, he's not worth the grief, you know that. Let him go.'

'Mr Harris is coming!' one of the kids yelled.

'Come on, Mitch,' Harley said.

I looked at Tim, looked into those piss-weak eyes and spat in his face.

'Break it up, boys,' I heard Mr Harris shout. 'Up to my office, Davies – now!'

Even though I'd felt those bones crack in my hands and seen the terror in his eyes I didn't feel any better. If anything, I felt a bit worse.

I sat in Harris's office wondering what my punishment would be. Detention, suspension? Who knew and who cared.

'Diana Richardson's CD player has been returned,' he said, walking into his office.

'But that doesn't mean for one minute that those kind of intimidation tactics are acceptable. Get it?'

'Yes, sir.'

'You know out of everyone in the whole year, it surprises me the most to see you out there fighting.' He gave me a long stare. 'It's very disappointing, you know?'

'Yes, sir.' Three bags full, sir.

'But I know what you're going through. I know about your grandfather being ill.'

'You do?' For some reason that shocked me.

'There are people out there who care about you, even if you don't think so.'

'Yes, sir.' Get me out of here!

'Get your feelings out in another way, Mitchell. You do that again and I'll call your mother. I'm sure that's the last thing she needs right now.'

'Thank you, sir.' And I was out of there before he changed his mind.

It was the talk around school. I did my best to ignore it, but Jed Travis just had to get in on the act. He came up to me the next afternoon when I was the only one at the lockers. 'You're a bit of a hero I hear? Protecting Miss Prissy Fuck.'

'Piss off, Travis,' I said.

'I hear you walk home from her house most mornings. Is that why you're not surfing? Too tired, discovered pussy instead? Bet Grandpa's not happy.'

I stared into my locker. When I turned around he was already walking away.

It was the first Sunday in November, which meant our surf club comp. It had only been three days since Jed Travis got in my ear and into my head. Paul had made it down to the beach to watch. He'd had a blood transfusion the day before and seemed to have a bit of energy – certainly enough to give me grief. He crapped on and on about how well Jed was surfing, and how he was going to video him, and that it still wasn't too late for him to enter Kirra. Blah, blah, blah.

I would've loved to have told Paul what he said to me and once I would have. But now I wasn't so sure who'd come out looking worse. Jed and I were competing against each other in the second heat. I felt sure that was a set-up too. The sun was shining, the wind was a light north-easterly, the swell was glassy and three to five feet. Even the water was quite warm for this time of year. So why did I feel so restless and agitated? Why couldn't I enjoy such a perfect day? What was wrong with me?

Jed got the first wave and carved some pretty good cutties, slashing off the top of the wave. He looked smug as he paddled back out. I went for the next one but didn't get on it.

'Bad luck,' mocked Jed.

It went on like this for the next fifteen minutes, Jed ripping it up, making the most of every opportunity, looking like a human frisbee as he mixed air into the rest of the wave. Even though he couldn't land it he still looked good. I heard Paul and some of the others cheering as he pulled each trick.

A three to four footer with real form came rolling in from nowhere. I knew the bell was about to go but I was in the best position and it was mine. I paddled hard, trying to find its rhythm and anticipate its every move. I felt aggro and drove the board hard, feeling the speed and power beneath my feet. I thought about what I had to do, my mind charging faster than my body. I centred my weight on my back foot and felt the take-off point. I cracked the lip and there I was, flying off into space. And I landed it – fucking perfectly.

They cheered me as I walked back up the beach. I could still feel the adrenaline pumping through my body. I shot a look at Jed and he snarled back. Had it been revenge that I was after? Because if it was, why didn't I feel the satisfaction I thought I would?

'That last move was well executed,' said Paul. 'The rest of it was pretty sloppy.'

I didn't answer.

'Just a word of advice,' he said.

I rolled my eyeballs and groaned just loud enough but he continued.

'Doing it out of anger doesn't usually feel that good. I suggest you try and do it using a more positive emotion. That's what separates the truly gifted from the try-hards.'

I swallowed hard and tried to act like I hadn't heard.

≈≈≈

There was one month of school till break-up. We'd all been made official Year 12s and were already copping the 'it's less than a year till the HSC' psych-up talk. The days were longer and starting to get hot. Every little grommet was surfing till dinner time. The Christmas ads were taking over the world, telling us it was 'the time to be happy'.

Paul was getting worse every day. I couldn't say exactly how, it was mostly little things like him staying inside all day, bruises appearing everywhere on his body, his small shuffling steps and the weight loss. He was literally disappearing. But the old girl still got him to light the gas barbie, like she did every night in summer as far back as I can remember. We'd sit down to steaks and chops and he'd sit there with a bit of mush on his plate that he never touched. It made me feel like we were playing this really pathetic game of let's pretend there's nothing wrong. The thing I couldn't get is, who were we playing it for?

As far as I could tell, Sue was the only other person who seemed to think it was strange, and one of those nights when I had half an eye on the telly I heard her and Mum arguing.

'Stop giving him that, that excuse for food.'

'Well, what's he going to eat?' said Mum.

'Nothing. He just picks when he feels like it.'

'Well, he likes to sit down as a family every night.'

'What? He does or you do?'

'Piss off, Sue,' said Mum. 'I'm only trying to do my best.'

'Look, he wants to sit down as a family to spend time with us, not eat. He stopped caring about that the day he decided to chuck it in.'

'I know.' I heard Mum start to cry. 'But how else am I going to get him and Mitch to talk and spend time together like they used to?'

'They will when they're ready, Liz.'

'But I'm scared that'll be too late.'

'Well, maybe Paul will wait until Mitch is ready. I've seen it happen before.'

'That's not fair,' whispered Mum. 'He's tired.'

I sat there feeling numb. It wasn't like I didn't feel anything, it was more like I felt too much. I knew Mum was talking about Paul when she said 'he's tired' but I was tired too. Tired of feeling pissed off and ripped off. I s'pose I wanted to feel like me again.

chapter nineteen

I looked at him and he smiled. His cheeks were hollow and his skin was nearly transparent but, I still recognised the eyes as his.

'You're a good boy, Mitch,' he whispered. 'You've always been a good boy, or man I should be saying now.'

We sat there absorbing the afternoon sun, enjoying the moment we had.

'I think that's why I knew I could bail,' he started. 'Because you were there, because I knew I could trust you.'

'I don't know if I can be as good as you,' I said, feeling the lump in my throat choking my words.

'You're better than me. You're great and never forget it. Never let anyone make you think otherwise. Do you understand?'

'Yes. Thank you.'

I picked up the phone and heard her scream, 'I got it!'

'Huh?'

Diana had never called me before and I was shocked to hear her voice on the other end of the line.

'I'm off to London,' she squealed. 'Can you believe it?'

'Yeah! That's fantastic. When did you find out?'

'Just then. I haven't told anyone yet. I wanted to tell you first.'

'You deserve it.'

'Oh my god, it's everything I've worked towards. All those early mornings, all those classes.'

'All those blisters,' I added, remembering how I'd bathed and bandaged her feet one night.

'Yeah,' she said. 'And you looked after me.'

We didn't say anything for a while. I thought about all those nights I'd stayed with her, just the two of us cocooned in our own little world, and it hurt. It physically hurt.

'Can you come over tonight – for dinner. It'll be me and Mum.'

'You mean I'm actually going to meet her?'

'Yeah,' Diana laughed. 'Is that OK?'

'Yeah, for sure.'

Dinner was good. It wasn't some fancy home-cooked meal, it was take-away Thai in the mega kitchen. Diana nearly lost it when her mother gave me directions to the toilet. I felt like telling her I probably knew this house better than she did. She was like Diana, or rather Diana was like her in that she was tall and fair haired with those grey eyes and dark eyebrows. But this woman trembled when she picked things up and never really looked at you when she spoke. She quietly sipped water, made the odd comment and then excused herself saying what a big day she'd had.

'She'll go and have a drink now,' Diana said. 'Poor thing. I feel sorry for her. I don't know what she's going to do when I'm gone.'

'Does it make you feel bad?'

'Yeah, but it's no good for me being here with her and maybe I'm no good for her. It's a pretty weird mother and daughter relationship isn't it? In fact the whole family's weird.'

'Show me a family who's not.' And this time I wasn't just trying to make her feel better. 'When are you going?'

'In two weeks. I want to have Christmas with my sister.'

'You'll miss the last day of school.'

'How tragic. What do you think you'll do for Christmas?'

'Not sure. I think it'll be a weird one this year, which I suppose fits in with the rest of the year.'

That night as we lay together and I breathed in the

scent of her body and felt her warmth and softness, I knew then I was ready to forgive and take the next jump.

ノノノ

There was a big end-of-year party at Reece's place. It was one of those still summer nights when you wonder how you're going to sleep. But we had it made as there was a pool and everyone was in full party mode. The guys were chucking the girls in, some were having water fights and the house was slowly being flooded. Couples who didn't get it together during the year were all over each other, the regulars were sitting around the bong and Tim was his usual pissed and red-faced self.

I was having a pretty good time but I couldn't say my heart was in it. It felt strange not being with her. I left the party and walked to the skate bowl, just as I had done months before.

Trevor was only just closing the milkbar and gave me a wave. Everything looked the same but it all felt so different. I traced my fingers around the initials D.R.

I thought about her and all her crazy tricks and it made me smile. How can a year be so bad and yet so incredible?

When I got home the local doctor was leaving. He had been over at night a couple of times before to give Paul a shot for pain. Paul was now refusing to go any-where near a hospital.

'Is he OK?' I asked Sue.

'He's just had some morphine,' she said.

I went into his room and saw him sleeping. Mum was sitting by him stroking his forehead.

'Good party, love?' she whispered.

'Yeah, it was OK,' I said. 'I think I'll go to bed.'

The next day Mum and Sue did some Chrissy shopping and I sat with Paul.

The day seemed like it had a pattern to it. He'd start to fall asleep, then wake up and say a few words. It was as though he realised there was something he'd forgotten to tell me. Then he'd fall back to sleep. All day it was the same. There was an old book by his bed. I picked it up and opened it to where a bookmark lay.

'Is that page 105?' he whispered. I had thought he was asleep.

'Yeah,' I said, glancing at the page number.

'It's my favourite. I made a copy of it for you. It's in that box I gave you.'

He sighed gently. 'Will you read it to me? The words are so special.'

I started to read a poem I had a vague memory of hearing as a child.

If you can keep your head when all about you
    Are losing theirs and blaming it on you;
If you can trust yourself when all men doubt you,
    But make allowance for their doubting too;
If you can wait and not be tired by waiting,
    Or, being lied about, don't deal in lies,

Or, being hated, don't give way to hating,
    And yet don't look too good, nor talk too wise.

If you can dream – and not make dreams your master;
    If you can think – and not make thoughts your aim;
If you can meet with triumph and disaster
    And treat those two impostors just the same;
If you can bear to hear the truth you've spoken
    Twisted by knaves to make a trap for fools,
Or watch the things you gave your life to broken,
    And stoop and build 'em up with worn out tools;

If you can make one heap of all your winnings
    And risk it on one turn of pitch-and-toss,
And lose, and start again at your beginnings
    And never breathe a word about your loss;
If you can force your heart and nerve and sinew
    To serve your turn long after they are gone,
And so hold on when there is nothing in you
    Except the will which says to them: 'Hold on';

If you can talk with crowds and keep your virtue,
    Or walk with kings – nor lose the common touch;
If neither foes nor loving friends can hurt you:
    If all men count with you, but none too much;
If you can feel the unforgiving minute
    With sixty seconds worth of distance run –

Paul cut in and with a whisper finished the last two
lines:

Yours is the Earth and everything that's in it,
    And – which is more – you'll be a man, my son!

chapter twenty

I guided his magic mal covered in frangipanis past the break and out to the horizon.

Young and old surfers, amateurs and professionals, those who only knew of him and those who knew him well paddled out with me. They made a circle. I looked at the boards of every size and dimension and the faces of the people who owned them.

Here we were in this vertical landscape of colours bobbing up and down on a smooth blue sea.

Simon Dobson and I pushed his mal into the middle of the circle I scattered the frangipanis around and set the board on fire. As I sat there and watched the board disintegrate I thought of what he had said to me only days ago.

'I'll be with you at Kirra. I mean not physically, but I'll be there with you. I might even hitch a ride on that stick of yours.'

He'd been gone nearly three months when Mum, Sue and I left for Kirra. I had thought I was going up on my own but Mum and Sue wanted to come too; in fact, they begged me. I said OK as long as they promised not to embarrass me in public. They promised. So we loaded up the car and set off on our journey.

I felt totally psyched. I was nervous but I was ready. The local daily had come over and taken a photo of me with my new board.

The caption read, "Mitchell Davies, 17, grandson of the late great longboard champion and board-shaper Paul Davies, gets ready to take on the surfing world at Kirra. The board Mitchell will be riding was the last board to be shaped by his grandfather. We wish him well."

Mum collected about a hundred copies of the paper just in case. Just in case of what? I wondered. But it was nice; she seemed pretty excited about the whole thing and I guess there were worse things to do than have a week off school up at the Gold Coast.

Mum had bought a new car – strict instructions of Paul's will – and it purred up the coast. We joked about the old Mazda and how it wouldn't have even made it to the end of our street. I sat there in the comfy seats and as the scenery gradually changed to a tropical paradise and the air became thicker, I felt the jitters start in my gut. Every now and then Mum would have to make a stop so I could run to the loo.

I'd sit there quietly saying to myself the things I knew Paul'd say. 'Stay focused. Play the moves in your head. Find the right spot on the board. Be in the right place at the right time. You'll only have that wave once. Don't be intimidated. And remember, it's meant to be fun.'

After driving on and off for nearly thirteen hours we arrived at the Gold Coast. Luckily I had the next day off before the contest started. I fell into my motel bed with my Walkman and a package. I was completely exhausted but there was something I'd been waiting to do. I had used all the self-control that was humanly possible not to open the package until I was alone. Now I ripped the bubble-wrap apart. A tape dropped out – it was from her. My hands fumbled as I tried to shove it wrong way around into the Walkman. At last I lay down, pushed play and closed my eyes.

There was her voice, but for real this time, playing in my head.

> *Hi, Mitch. It's me, Diana. It's weird talking into one of these things but I don't think I'm good at letter writing. Well, you're probably off to Kirra in a couple of days. I'll be thinking of you and I know your grandpa would be too. I think he was very proud. You're lucky to have had someone who cared so much for you. I'm sure that's why you're such a wonderful person and why you could care for me so much. You must miss him a lot.*

Listen to me, I'm crapping on and being all serious. I don't think I'm very good at speaking into these things either. Maybe I'll try a phone-call next.

London's freezing and the classes are heavy going but it's great being here with my sister. I showed her a photo of you and she said you were very cute. I miss you and although I know last year was very hard for you it was very special for me. I'll always remember it as the year I met a great friend.

Oh no – crapping on again. I'm about to say goodbye but don't turn the tape off as I'm going to record the music by Grieg that I played for you. Listen to it before you go out there to compete. It'll give you strength. I remember how peaceful and happy that music made you feel – at least that was one thing I could give you.

Thank you for keeping my secrets. I love you and I miss you and your beautiful shoulders and your smooth back. Oh dear, I better go before I say too much. Bye.'

But she had said too much and there was only one thing I could do about it.

The locals were pretty used to this sort of thing, as some of the world's best surfers lived around there. The junior contest pulled big crowds and lots of chicks in bikinis. It's good having the contest there. Even if Kirra's not happening, there are still another half-dozen breaks to choose from and the contest shifts there. But it wasn't my problem to sweat on the conditions, it was my problem to make the most of what it had to offer.

Finally I woke up to the morning of March the fifth, a day I felt at times I would never see but here I was, a little bit older and a lot wiser. I never would've believed it if someone had told me I wouldn't be here with Paul. My life of surfing without Paul was an equation I had never considered, probably because I didn't think I could do it. But now, after everything, I knew I could. Is this what he had been preparing me for?

I'd had a good session surfing the day before. Being a natural footer gave me an advantage here. I also got to spend some time studying a piece of coast I was not familiar with. It was good preparation and now I just wanted to get in the water.

The swell was four to five feet, with the odd big one coming in. The wind was a light south-westerly and now the tide was out there were some nice waves breaking off the point. I put on my singlet and waited for my first heat. I had fluked no locals in this one, so I was happy.

I hate just sitting there and waiting. It's when my

mind starts playing tricks on me and I have to concentrate hard to pull it back into line and focus on
what I'm about to do.

The talent was good. There were a couple of guys
out there who were totally ripping, but on the whole
I'd say it was pretty even. By the time they'd called
my heat the swell had dropped a bit, but man was it
fun out there. My turns were smooth and slick, and I
carved some big backhand manoeuvres. I managed to
land a couple of little airs OK, which felt good. I won
my heat and the heart really started pumping.
Winning my heat meant I skipped the second heat and
was a starter for the third and final.

I went up and saw Mum and Sue, who were man-
aging to keep a comfortable distance from me as
promised. They were pretty excited for me but I don't
think they really had a clue. The atmosphere was
pumping – heaps of people, good music and sponsor
reps swarming around. I wanted to get amongst it but
I could feel the jitters returning. Some of the local
boys were displaying incredible talent with good
mixed routines and there was one grom who was
simply barrel prone.

I got my Walkman and went and found a quiet
spot. I sat there and listened to the music Diana had
sent me.

I didn't want to think about her and the times
we'd had. I wanted to think about where I was now
and how lucky I was to be there.

Some official tapped me on the shoulder.

'Are you Mitch Davies?'

'Yeah,' I answered.

'Well, you better get out there, the final's starting.'

I bolted down to the sand and grabbed my board. The others were already in the water. As I paddled frantically I tried to steady my nerves. 'Don't blow it now. Focus. Focus,' I whispered to myself.

Two guys had already scored their first. I watched and waited, trying not to panic and get on just anything. I wanted to wait for my wave.

Then I saw it coming – it was almost screaming at me. I swung around and started paddling. I knew I needed to make the drop. I drove hard down its fast-peeling wall, did a clean bottom turn and pulled straight into a barrel. I gave it a few pumps and got deep inside, standing up with head room to spare. I skidded my palm across its back wall and watched the blue curtain spilling over me.

I was in there for maybe six seconds but I had a sensation that time had stopped. And just for that moment I sensed him there and smelt the dust and tobacco on his hands. I laughed and screamed as I came shooting out of the tube. My victory tunnel. This was what he'd prepared me for.